SADDLE SHOE BLUES

CARROLL HOFELING MORRIS

Deseret Book Company
Salt Lake City, Utah

First printing March 1987
Second printing April 1987

Library of Congress Cataloging-in-Publication Data

Morris, Carroll Hofeling.
    Saddle shoe blues.

    Summary: Growing up in the 1950's, a young Mormon
girl copes with a reading disability and becomes friends
with a girl from a poor family.
    [1. Friendship—Fiction. 2. Reading—Fiction.
3. Mormons—Fiction] I. Title.
PZ7.M827244Sad 1987   [Fic]   87-595
ISBN 0-87579-077-1

For J. and L.,
because I never forgot

CHAPTER ONE

"Lor-etta Miller, what have you done to your shoes!"

I tucked my right foot behind my left, but by then it was too late. Momma had seen the scuffed toe of my brand new saddle shoe.

"You've been riding that bike with no brakes again, haven't you? And in your new shoes!"

"I didn't mean to. I forgot about the brakes, and when I wanted to stop, my foot just went down like it always does . . ."

Momma shook her head. "Well, get in here and see what you can do to make it look a little better. It's time to polish shoes for Sunday, anyway."

Momma hated scuffed shoes. Every Saturday, I had to shine mine with Johnson's shoe polish, the kind that's supposed to be good for white baby shoes. After they dried, I had to buff them to as much of a shine as they were willing to give. If they didn't look good enough, or if I got white polish on the black insets, I had to do them over again.

I did my shoes twice the Saturday before my first day of school. I wouldn't have had to polish them at all if I hadn't worn them when I went bike riding on the road out in front of our farm. Momma had told me to leave them in the box until school started, but I couldn't bear not to put them on. They were my first pair of new shoes ever. I had an older sister and a momma who kept everything, so I had been in shoes for six years without ever having a pair that didn't start out on Cheryl first.

With polish in hand, I tried to make the right shoe look like it had when I took it out of the box, shiny and perfect, smelling like the inside of the Shoe and Saddle Shop. I couldn't. It just didn't look the same anymore, not even after Cheryl helped me polish and buff it a second time.

By the time Momma passed inspection on my shoes, the other kids had already finished. There was a line of shiny shoes marching down the oilcloth-covered kitchen table. That was the only part of Momma's Saturday shoe-shining ritual I liked: looking at the line of shoes that went from my baby brother Joe's itsy-bitsy oxfords to my biggest brother Alma's huge ones.

In between were my saddle shoes and white strap Sunday shoes, Lorenzo's oxfords, then Cheryl's saddle shoes and black patent leather Sunday shoes. She got to wear black patent because she was older. She was thirteen, almost old enough to wear high heels to church.

Sometimes, Momma made the boys clean up their cowboy boots, too. They really hollered about that, 'cause they knew that the boots would be all messy again as soon as they wore them out to the corral. But Momma was like that, and the boys always ended up doing what she said.

Of all us kids, only Joe and I had names we could shorten. Alma was always Alma, Lorenzo was always Lorenzo, and Cheryl never got called anything else. I've always been called Letty, which is fine with me. I never did like the name Loretta. The only person who called me that was Momma, especially when she was mad or she wanted something. Then it was "Lor-etta!"

"Lor-etta! You're still in bed! If you don't get up right now and get yourself ready for breakfast, you'll be late for the bus. And on your very first day of school."

"I'm sick, Momma," I said. "I feel like I'm going to throw up."

"It's nothing but nerves. Come on now, get dressed. I want to take your picture after you eat."

The first day of every school year, Momma always herded all the school-age kids out on the back lawn to take their picture in front of the pine trees. I knew I couldn't get out of that, so I crawled from the warm nest I had made for myself and got dressed in my new school clothes.

The corduroy skirt and vest Momma had made just for me were out of a brown plaid that had lots of gold and some orange in it. I can still remember the texture of the corduroy and the number of brass buttons that filed down the front of the vest. I can still feel the nauseating mixture of excitement and fear I had as my momma pushed the button on her Brownie Hawkeye. The snapshot captured my fright; the rebellion of my wild, naturally curly hair, which I had flattened down with water as much as I could; and my stick legs rising up out of anklets and those saddle shoes.

There were four of us Millers in the first-day-of-school picture taken early in September of 1951, and we all looked alike. We had Momma's big smile and funny-colored eyes that were mostly blue, with a yellow ring right in the center. We had her curly hair and golden skin. The only thing that was different about us was our hair color (some had blond hair and some brown) and our size. Daddy, who had plain blue eyes, thin lips, and skin that sunburned real easy, must have felt left out.

"Get going, Letty!" Lorenzo said, pushing me from behind as soon as Momma had taken the picture.

"Momma, do I have to ride the bus? Can't you take me just today?"

"I have too much to do. I have to stay home with Joe, and I want to get another twenty-four quarts of tomatoes

3

canned." She knelt in front of me and smoothed back the brown curls that had already sprung up again. "You'll be all right. Lorenzo will show you which classroom you're in. Won't you, Lorenzo?"

"Just hope Old Lady Reigert isn't teaching first grade this year. She's mean."

"Really?" I asked.

"Really."

"Will you take her?" interrupted Momma. She wanted an answer.

"Yeah. I'll take her, but she better hurry, 'cause I want to catch the bus on the way out."

Momma shook her head. "I might have known. Okay. Here's your school bag, Letty." The bag she handed me was red-and-white plaid with a little blue stripe. It had a black plastic handle and black plastic closures on the front. "And your lunch money," she added, handing me a quarter. "Put it in the inside pocket."

"But hurry!" called Lorenzo, who was already walking toward the road. I glared at him and put the quarter in the little pocket as quickly as my shaking fingers could manage.

"Good luck." Momma kissed me, then gave me a little shove in the direction Lorenzo had gone. After one more desperate hug, I followed Lorenzo out through the front gate to the road.

We lived way out in the country. The black road in front of our farm went east and west. East to the mountains where the sun came up, and west into town. Lorenzo wanted to catch the bus on its way out to the last stop, instead of waiting for it to pull up in front of our farm on the way back in.

The last stop was the Knotts place. Their house was down a long dirt road that had a real big bump in it. Lorenzo wanted to be sitting on the very back seat when the bus went over that bump. "It's the closest thing we've got to a carnival ride," he always said. He had learned about the bump from Cheryl, but she didn't catch the bus on the way out anymore. Neither did Alma.

I couldn't wait to see what going over that bump was like. For as long as I could remember, my brothers and sister had talked about it.

Just then, the bus came up over the hill. It stopped right in front of us with a familiar screech, and Lorenzo disappeared inside. My stomach lurched as I put my foot on the bottom step of the bus. I was on my way, and not at all sure I wanted to be.

"Well, if it isn't Letty. I thought you might be joining us."

"Bishop Hansen!"

The bus driver laughed and held out his hand. I shook it, just like I always did in church. It seemed funny to be shaking hands on the school bus with the bishop of our ward. (We were Mormons.) It seemed funny to see him sitting behind the steering wheel dressed in jeans and a checked shirt instead of sitting on the stand in a suit and tie. "Hope you like the bump," he said as I started back to Lorenzo.

Lorenzo was already sitting on the very last seat, the one that ran across the back of the bus. I sat down beside him. "All right, it's not too far now," he said as the bus started down the Knotts lane. "Better grab on, 'cause it's going to throw you right up in the air."

I grasped the metal bar that ran above the seat in front of me and held my breath. Nothing happened.

"I thought you said it wasn't far!"

"It's coming right up. We're getting closer . . . closer . . . Now!"

I went flying into the air and came down hard on the seat.

"Wasn't that great?" Lorenzo asked. Then he saw my face. "For Pete's sake, Letty, what's the matter with you?"

"I'm going to throw up."

Lorenzo's eyes were right up in my face. "Don't you dare!" he commanded.

I clamped my lips together and drew a deep, shuddery breath through my nose; I was afraid to open my mouth. I loved Lorenzo. He was five years older than I was, but he was my best friend. If Lorenzo said not to throw up, I wasn't about to throw up.

He must have understood how I was feeling, because he started talking to me to get my mind off of the stuff pressing against my Adam's apple.

"You've never been to the Knotts place before, have you?"

I shook my head.

"You're in for a surprise. You've never seen anything like it."

"What's the matter with it? And what's the matter with them? Why does Momma say we mustn't play with them?"

"They're poor. Real poor. And . . . well, you'll see."

What did he mean? I'd seen Mr. Knotts and the Knotts boys before, and they looked okay to me. They weren't crunched into grotesque shapes, like Uncle Orvel. They didn't have great purple splotches on their faces, like the man who stood behind the counter in the Feed and Seed Store. They didn't have a claw where a hand should have been, like the man at the John Deere place.

I never did get to see that claw straight on. I wanted to, but I was always too scared to just look at it nice and natural, the way my Daddy did. He never acted like there was anything different about the man. But to me, the cold metal that could click around something the way an eagle's claw snatches a mouse was a horrible mystery.

When the Knotts kids got on the bus, I looked them over real close, but I still couldn't tell what was the matter with them. Whatever it was, it didn't jump right out at me.

"See," whispered Lorenzo to me, "that first boy is Bob. He's in Cheryl's class. He can beat the stuffing out of everybody."

"He's too tall to be in eighth grade. He's as tall as Alma and Alma is in twelfth."

"Bob had to stay behind a couple of times, stupid. Here comes Henry now. Ugh. He still has ringworm."

I followed Lorenzo's gaze to a shaved-off spot on Henry's head. It had an ugly sore in the middle of it.

"It's catching, so don't touch it," instructed Lorenzo.

I shook my head solemnly.

The last Knotts to board the bus was a little girl.

"That's Dinah. She didn't ride the bus last year. That means she's a first-grader. She'll be in your class."

"How do you know so much about them?"

Lorenzo shrugged. "You hear stuff. And Henry was in my class when we started out, but he has to do fourth grade again this year."

Bob, Henry, and Dinah Knotts sat down in the middle of the bus. Then they all turned around and looked at me and Lorenzo. It made me feel awful funny, them looking at us without saying anything, or even nodding. I guess we were looking at them the same way.

Something else about them hit me at the same time as the smell, and I thought I understood what Lorenzo had been trying to say. It wasn't the jeans with the holes in the knees or the dirty smudges on Dinah's dress or the socks that sagged at the heels. It wasn't the way Henry wiped his nose with the back of his hand and rubbed it on the green seat.

It was a look in their eyes that I'd never noticed before.

That look made me think of the old coyote Daddy and I caught sneaking around the chicken coop. In the moment before the coyote ran, he looked right at me. "Poor coyote," I had said. "He was just hungry, Daddy. And scared."

"Maybe so," my daddy replied, patting my shoulder. "But we can't hand him a chicken every time he comes around. If he's the one that's been causing the problems around here, he's an old hand at stealing. We'll have to shoot him."

I was still thinking about the coyote when the bus stopped at our place again, this time to pick up Cheryl and Alma. They were too old to like the bump anymore. They were too old for Lorenzo and me, I guess, because they sat up front and didn't even act like we were there. I was real glad to have Lorenzo sitting beside me.

He must have known, because he let me hold his hand when we went into the red brick building that said *Elementary School, Pryor Creek, Wyoming* over the door. Lorenzo told Momma later that he was dragging me. He might have been—he had to pry my fingers off when we got to my room.

"This is it," he said, shoving me inside.

I walked into a new world that day, a world full of wonders.

Like chairs and tables just the right size.

Like the big round thing in the girls bathroom that looked like a fancy watering trough. When you pressed down on the bar with your foot, water came out in a spray all around. And there was a button to push for pink soap that smelled good and clean.

Like milk in little glass jars that, except for their size, looked just like the regular quart-size milk jars. You lifted a tab and put a straw in and sucked the cool, rich deliciousness into your mouth—slowly, while the teacher read from a book.

But I also walked into a world that included Dinah Knotts. For six years, she was either right beside me or in front of me. For six years, it was the same in every class I had. The teacher would say, "Knotts, Dinah. You sit here, Dinah. Miller, Loretta. Yes, I'll call you Letty. You sit next to Dinah, Letty."

I had never seen Dinah before that day, in spite of the fact that her place wasn't that far from ours. Especially if you walked down the ditch at the head of the alfalfa field instead of going out to the road and then back up their lane. But by the time I took my assigned seat, I had already decided that Momma's opinion of the Knotts family was right. All it took was one good look at Dinah.

Her hair was matted in clumps, and so dirty I couldn't tell for sure if it was blond or light brown. She looked too pale, like she didn't get enough sun, and there were dark circles under her eyes. Her dress looked like something she had picked out of the laundry pile.

And her shoes! As I compared her old, run-down saddle shoes to my nearly new and neatly polished shoes, I sighed with relief.

I was nothing like Dinah Knotts.

CHAPTER TWO

The year I started first grade, there were 2517 people in Pryor Creek. At least that's what the sign said. "Pryor Creek City Limits. Pop. 2517." I didn't know what that many people all in one place would look like, but I knew one thing for sure: there were more cows than people in our part of Wyoming. My daddy's double S brand alone was on fifteen hundred head. Add up a few more herds, and people were way down on the tally sheet.

I guess that's why Momma and Daddy taught us kids that being friendly was important. They always spoke to people we passed on the street when we were in town. They took their time when they were doing business in Main Street Drug or the Shoe and Saddle Shop. Whenever we met a car on the road, whoever was driving our car waved their right hand as a greeting—whether they knew the other driver or not.

Daddy liked to tell the story about an Eastern feller who had come to northern Wyoming looking for a ranch to buy. He asked Daddy to help him find a likely place, so for a week or more Daddy drove him all around. Every time they passed another car or truck, Daddy would wave. After a while, the feller asked, "Do you know all those people?"

"Nope," Daddy answered. "Just our way of letting each other know we're not alone out here."

I understood that story, even though I was just a kid. Long before I went to school, I knew what lonely felt like. Our place was a good fifteen miles out of town, not too far from the open range. I couldn't just walk around the block or down the street if I wanted someone to play with. I had to rely on my brothers and sister for company.

They weren't that interested in playing with me, to tell the truth. My big brother Alma was already so old he was almost grown up. Cheryl was old enough to know how to talk just like a mother already, and I didn't need two of those. Joe was fun to play with when he was a baby, but when Momma made watching him one of my chores, it wasn't so much fun anymore. That left Lorenzo. And even Lorenzo didn't always want me hanging around.

That's why I always liked it when we had unexpected visitors, especially if they had their kids along. When that happened, Momma would invite them in and set extra plates on the table. If Daddy was working nearby, he'd come in and sit a spell, sucking on his toothpick while he and our company talked over stock prices, how much rain we'd had, and whether or not there'd be good pheasant hunting come fall. Us kids would scatter the minute the adults got busy talking, and we'd play until Momma called us in to eat.

More than once after such a visit, Daddy said, "Sure is a nice thing to have neighbors." I always thought that was strange, because the Knottses were our nearest neighbors, and Momma never set extra plates at the table for them. Oh, they did come over once in a while, but it was always for a reason, never just for company.

Henry and Bob Knotts only came over when they wanted to collect their bounty for killing "varmits." Daddy was the treasurer for the "Varmit" Control Board, so he was the one who paid out. If you brought in a pair of mag-pie feet, you got a nickle. If you brought in all four feet of a bobcat or coyote, you got a whole fifteen dollars. The Knotts boys were Daddy's best customers. He paid out more money to them than he did to Alma and Lorenzo, and my two brothers were crack shots.

Mr. Knotts came over even more often than Henry and Bob. He and Daddy had worked out a deal: Mr. Knotts could use Daddy's tools if he would help keep our equipment in running order. He was good at that. "Asa is a wonder, Faye," Daddy would say. "I suppose it comes from necessity. He can't afford to buy a new part every time his equipment breaks down. He has to figure out some way to fix it himself, and most of the time, he does. Saved me many a trip to town, Asa has."

To tell the truth, I think Daddy liked Mr. Knotts more than Momma approved of. I remember once when the Knottses' cows got through the fence and into our alfalfa field. Mr. Knotts came over to see what Daddy wanted to do about the ruined field and the repairs on the fence. Daddy helped him fix the fence and let it go at that. When Momma asked him why, he said, "Because two of Asa's cows and a heifer died of the bloat. Our alfalfa will grow back, but Asa's cows won't get up and walk."

So I had seen the Knotts men more than once, but never the Knotts women. Dinah came as a total surprise to me. I had had no idea that Bob and Henry had a little sister, until the moment she set foot in the bus the first day of school. As for Mrs. Knotts, I guess I always figured there was one—somewhere. I mean, if there were Knotts kids, there had to be a Mrs. Knotts, right? But I never laid eyes on her until we went up the mountain for one last fishing trip the fall of 1951.

We drove part way up the Big Horns and pulled into a campground that had a lot of pine trees and a small, bubbling creek nearby. Daddy and the boys were going to drive farther on up to fish the larger, willow-lined creeks the next morning.

"We'll be getting up early, so you don't have to worry about feeding us before we go," Daddy told Momma.

"I didn't intend to. I expect you to bring some trout back for breakfast."

Daddy grinned. "Right."

"Can I go with?" I asked. If Lorenzo was going, I wanted to go.

"Not this time, sweetie. This time it's just the boys."

"I don't want to stay in camp!"

"I'll take you out tomorrow evening," Daddy promised.

Usually, there's lots to do in the morning when you camp out. It's cold when you wake up, and you have to build a fire real quick so you can make hot chocolate. After the fire burns down, you can fry potatoes nice and brown in a cast iron skillet. But this time, Momma just gave us bread-and-on-it. Bread-and-on-it was bread and whatever topping we could find. I had bread and cheese first, then bread and jam. I figured that would hold me till Daddy and the boys got home with their trout.

By ten o'clock, the sun was way up in the sky, and it was hot. Cheryl had put on her swimming suit and was sunning herself on a big rock, like a lizard. Momma had spread out a blanket in the shade of a pine tree and was lying down with Joe, trying to get him to take a nap. That left me with nobody to play with and nothing to do.

I walked over to the creek and sat down on a flat rock. For a while, I busied myself watching the bubbles that got caught in a pool by my rock. Then I dangled my fingers in the water. It felt cool and delicious.

Momma never let us go barefoot, so I was wearing anklets and my saddle shoes. Inside those shoes and socks, my feet were burning. They ached to be free and in the icy water. I gave Momma a sideward glance to see if she was still sleeping. Then I took my shoes and socks off.

I was just about to put my feet into the water when Momma said, "Lor-etta, I thought I told you to stay back from the stream."

"Can't I just put my feet in the water? I'll stay on this rock."

Momma raised up on one elbow. After a moment, she said, "All right. But only if you promise not to move off that rock." I promised. Then I plunged my feet into the creek.

"Ahhhh!"

"What's the matter?" cried Momma.

"Nothing. The water's cold, that's all."

"Better stay out of it, then."

"No. It feels too good."

It did, after the first shock. Of course, that might have been because my feet were numb. They didn't feel anything at all. It was like they didn't even belong to me.

They were red up to my ankle when I finally pulled them out. I sat on the rock and watched them as the red faded and they began to tingle and then to warm up. When the heat from the rock and the sun made them nice and hot again, I stuck them back into the water.

I sat there, alternately freezing and baking my feet, until it got boring. But I wasn't bored long. Just as I was about to put my shoes and socks on, I heard something coming up the road.

It was the Knotts family's old pickup. It rattled and coughed and kicked up red dust as it came into the campground. It turned at a fork and went a little way up the other side of the creek before it stopped with a wheeze.

The doors flew open. From the cab and the back of the pickup, the whole family bailed out. There weren't that many of them, but their energy reminded me of a swarm leaving a hornet's nest. Behind me, I heard Momma groan, "Oh no."

On the opposite side of the creek, they began setting up camp. If you could call it that. The meadow—which moments ago had been a clean, neat expanse of green—was now covered with an odd assortment of things. They had appeared so suddenly that it was as if the meadow had sprouted boxes and sacks and piles of stuff the way a garden sprouts weeds.

I couldn't help but wonder what Momma thought of that. Our camp was neat and clean. She even had us pick up stray pieces of wood and pinecones. I was always surprised and relieved that she didn't make us rake or sweep the dirt around the campfire.

Mrs. Knotts didn't seem worried about such things at all. She just flopped down on a bench and closed her eyes. She was a big lady, almost as big as Mr. Knotts. She wore a handkerchief on her head. Wisps of grayish hair had escaped and framed her face, which was round and sort of flat. Over her dress she wore an apron. It was dirty.

I felt silly, sitting on the rock watching them, but they were fascinating. They seemed to be going in all directions. They hollered. They shouted. They tossed things out the back of the pickup. They were so busy that they were totally unaware I was watching them.

That is, until Mr. Knotts headed my way with a net full of bottles. I knew what he had in mind, because Momma had already put our pop bottles in the creek so they would stay cold. Only the bottles Mr. Knotts was carrying sure didn't look like Coca Cola or Nesbitt orange or Dr. Pepper bottles.

When I realized what they were, my mouth dropped open.

They were beer bottles.

Drinking beer was a terrible thing, Momma always said. If that was true, I figured anyone who did it must also be terrible.

Suddenly, Mr. Knotts looked strange and threatening. I scrambled to my feet, but I was too late.

"Howdy," said Mr. Knotts as he situated the dark brown bottles in the creek. His booming voice had a funny, soft edge to it.

"Hello."

"You're the little Miller gal, ain't ya?"

I nodded.

"All your men gone fishing?"

I nodded.

"They got a head start on us then. But ain't nobody can outfish the Knotts. That's what they say back in the Smoky Mountains. Ain't nobody can outfish the Knotts— or outshoot."

I felt like I had to say something, so I ventured, "Your boys bring over more magpie feet than anybody else."

"What'd I tell ya?"

While we were talking, Dinah had been sideling up behind her daddy. "This here's my little gal Dinah," Mr. Knotts said, pulling her out from behind him. "But I reckon you already know that, seeings how y'all are in the same class."

I nodded.

"Come on, Pa!" Henry hollered.

"Got to get going," Mr. Knotts said, touching his hat with one big hand. "Nice to meet you . . ." He paused, waiting for me to tell him my name.

"Letty."

"Letty. That's a nice name. Sounds Southern."

16

"It's short for Loretta."

"It's right purty. You two gals mind the camp, now."

In a great whirl of shouting and throwing and gathering, Mr. Knotts and the two boys got back into the pickup and drove out onto the main road. Mrs. Knotts spread out a blanket and lay down. That left Dinah with nobody to play with and nothing to do.

Dinah and I stared across the creek at each other. I had been wishing I had somebody to play with, and I could tell by the look on Dinah's face that she wanted to play. But from where I sat on my side of the creek, she seemed too far away. We might as well have had the Big Horn River between us.

Behind me, I heard a noise. I turned to see Momma starting to pack our things.

"Come help," she said. "If we get things together, we'll be ready to load the pickup when your daddy comes back."

That night, we moved to a different campground higher up the mountain. The fishing would be better and Daddy wouldn't have to drive so far, Momma said.

But I knew better.

CHAPTER THREE

About Thanksgiving, I found out that I was more like Dinah Knotts than I wanted to be.

We were both dumb. I was dumb at reading, and Dinah was just plain dumb. At least it seemed that way. She never said anything unless the teacher asked her, and then she answered in such a soft voice that Mrs. Bennington thought she answered wrong even when she answered right.

I had no inkling that I was dumb the first day of school, or even the first few weeks. School was fun, then. We played some games, sang songs, listened to the teacher read, and started learning the alphabet and our numbers.

I was great at reciting. I remembered everything the teacher told us, and I learned to say the alphabet just like that. Reading it was something else again.

From the very moment that Mrs. Bennington started drilling us on the alphabet cards that stretched across the top of the blackboard in the front of the room, I realized the alphabet was a mystery.

The world was full of mysteries, I already knew that. Mysteries were things that everyone understood but me. Some of them I could figure out after a while, like what made Momma mad, and what I needed to do to make her happy.

Others weren't so easy, like what made one year change into the next. One day, it was 1950. The next, it was 1951. Not knowing how that happened bothered me, but nobody else seemed to wonder. They just went on doing what they always did.

The alphabet was one of those mysteries I couldn't figure out. It was easy enough when Mrs. Bennington held up the cards in the order we had learned to say them, but when she mixed them up, I had no idea what was going on. There was no message in the lines that made sense to me.

But everybody else got it.

Billy Bucher of the blond cowlick and freckly face got it. So did knobby-kneed Gloria Nesbitt.

And Janet Banks, who had cheeks like a Kewpie doll.

Stevie McClenahan got it, of course. Stevie was . . . well, to my first-grade eyes, Stevie was *fine*.

Clyde Robertson got it, and he had flunked first grade the year before.

After a while, even Dinah got it. But I didn't.

Before a month was out, it got to be a joke, waiting to see what stupid thing I was going to say when the teacher asked me a question.

"What is this letter, Letty?" asked Mrs. Bennington one day in her stuffy-nose voice.

The card she held before me had a shape on it that consisted of a circle and a line, so I knew it was either *B* or *D* or *P*, but I couldn't tell which, because it wouldn't hold still. It looked like it was floating and turning around in circles at the same time.

"Letty?"

I shook my head. I was waiting for the letter to hold still, so I could tell her what it was. Otherwise, I'd have to guess.

"What is it now?" Mrs. Bennington was getting impatient.

I guessed. "Uh . . . *B?*"

With a sigh and a shrug, she gave up on me. "Which letter is it, Dinah?"

"It's a *P*," Dinah said softly.

"Speak up so I can hear you," ordered Mrs. Bennington.

"*P!*" Dinah fairly shouted.

I hated it when Dinah could tell what the secret letter was. It made me even madder when she started whispering the answers to me from the corner of her mouth. "*D.* It's a *D.*"

"Show off," I said one day after she tried to help me.

"I just didn't want the teacher to get mad at you."

"You stay out of it. I don't need your help!" I kicked at the playground gravel, which scuffed the toe of my shoe and only made me madder. "Besides, you talk funny."

"I don't either."

"Yes you do. Your words come out slow. And you say y'all."

"What's so funny about that?"

"Nobody I know says it but you."

"My ma and pa do."

It suddenly occurred to me that I hadn't seen her momma since our trip up the mountain. "How come I never see your momma?"

"How come I never see yours?"

"I dunno. You can come see her anytime. She's most always home."

"Same goes for you. Ma works in town, but Pa's always somewhere around the place. All you gotta do is come over."

"I could, I guess."

"But you won't. My pa says where he comes from folks are more neighborly. He says if we still lived there, we'd have lots of company, 'specially on weekends."

"Don't you ever have company?"

"Nope. Nobody ever comes down our lane just to visit."

My toe was busy in the gravel.

"I'd like it if you could play, sometime," Dinah said softly. "You could get off the bus at our house and keep me company for a while. And I could help you with the alphabet."

"I told you, I don't need your help."

"We could just play together, then. The boys go out to help Pa after we get home, and I get lonesome by myself."

"Isn't your momma there when you get home?"

"She doesn't get home till late. She's a presser at the laundry."

I had been to the Pryor Creek Laundry once, and I never wanted to go back again. It was one big room filled with machines and tables. I couldn't breathe, it was so hot in there, and the machines made terrible noises when they let off bursts of steam.

"Does she like working there?" I asked.

"No. But she has to. Pa don't make much money on the Rock Pile."

"On the what?"

Dinah dropped her eyes. "That's what we call our farm."

They weren't the only ones who called it the Rock Pile. I found that out at supper. We were passing around the bowls of mashed potatoes, flour gravy, green beans, and sliced tomatoes, when Daddy said, "I talked to Asa Knotts today."

"What about?" asked Momma, passing on the beans.

"Maybe running some of his cattle with ours."

"Do you think that's a good idea?"

"Now, Mother. Don't be too hard on Asa. He does the best he can with what he's got." Daddy shook his head. "I don't know how he manages to make a living on the Rock Pile."

"Why does everybody call it that, Daddy?" I asked.

" 'Cause that's what it is, honey. The rocks Asa turns up each spring are the best crop he gets all year. Too bad there's no market for them."

Alma and Lorenzo laughed.

"Every spring I can remember, Bob has taken some time off school," said Alma. "You ask him why, and he always says, 'Got to pick rock.' "

Lorenzo shoved his food over to one side of his mouth. "Henry, too. Wish I could use that excuse."

"Don't talk with your mouth full," said Momma absently. She was trying to get Joe to stop playing with his potatoes.

"How come we don't have as many rocks as they do?" I asked. "Their place is right next to ours."

Daddy leaned back on his chair. "Just a matter of geography. It's like somebody drew a line right where our alfalfa field ends and their farmyard begins. The land drops off pretty sharp right there. The ground is sandier and more hilly. And there's that wash running north and south through their place."

"If it's so bad, how come they stay there?"

"It's a poor man's place, honey," said Daddy. He sucked on his toothpick thoughtfully. "Only a poor man would buy it, and once he's on it, he's bound to stay poor. No matter how hard Asa works, there's no way to get a good crop off the Rock Pile, so he's always in debt. Running a few cattle can't make up for that. Even when he gets a good price for them."

"Why don't they move?"

"When you're poor, you don't have many options," said Daddy.

"What does that mean?"

"Means you don't have many choices," said Lorenzo.

Lorenzo liked showing off.

"Dinah asked me if I would get off the bus at her house sometimes."

"She what?" asked Momma, looking at me sharply.

"She's there all by herself after school, and she wants some company."

"Sounds like a nice—" began Daddy, but Momma interrupted.

"I hope you told her I wouldn't allow it."

"Faye—"

"If we allow Letty to get off the bus at Dinah's, there'll be *two* unsupervised children instead of just one. That's no improvement."

"Maybe Dinah could come here," I suggested.

"Lor-etta, we have as little to do with her family as possible. They're not bad people, but they aren't the sort we associate with." Momma shook her head. "I declare, sometimes I don't know what's going on in your head."

What was going on in my head was this: I needed somebody to help me learn the alphabet, and I had decided that Dinah was the best choice. That way, I wouldn't have to admit to anyone in my family that I was having trouble.

When I told Momma about Dinah's suggestion, I was doing what Daddy called "testing the waters." I knew from Momma's response that getting off the bus at Dinah's house was out.

CHAPTER FOUR

It was too bad Momma didn't let me go visit Dinah. She might have been able to help me with my problem. But Momma didn't, so Dinah couldn't. I was left on my own.

I started studying those alphabet cards real hard, and I finally learned some of them. But others, like the *P* and *D* and *B*, were still too hard for me. So I studied the cards some more, and I found some secrets that helped.

Almost every card had something on it that was different. The *O* card had a black mark on the edge. The *Q* didn't. That's how I could tell the *Q* and *O* apart. The upper right-hand corner of the *B* card was bent, and the *D* had a little wrinkle through the middle. After I realized that, I could tell which was which without getting them mixed up with the *P*.

I felt pretty good about that, until Mrs. Bennington started putting the letters together to make words. Then I had to start all over again, finding secret clues on each word card. It worked out pretty good, but I sure thought it was a dumb way to teach, leaving it up to the kids to figure out what the clues were themselves.

I might have started hating school if I hadn't been doing great in math and other things. Even though Lorenzo needed to push me through the door the first day, I had gone into Mrs. Bennington's first-grade class ready to learn everything. I didn't have any idea it would be so hard to read. Lorenzo and Alma weren't crazy about reading, but they did okay. Cheryl loved to read, especially *True Confessions* magazine. She kept it hidden underneath her bed.

I knew only one person in my family who couldn't read and that was Uncle Orvel. Even then, everybody just figured that a scrunched mind came with a scrunched body. They didn't give much thought to it. "That's just Orvel," they said. "He can't help it."

I didn't tell Momma I was having trouble. It seemed to me that she was embarrassed that Uncle Orvel was her brother. She didn't like having to explain about him. See, Momma liked everything to be just right, and she got upset when it wasn't. I knew she wouldn't be happy finding out I was like Uncle Orvel.

I managed to keep it a secret until we started reading out of *Dick and Jane*. Then, everything I had figured out on the word cards and sentence cards didn't work anymore. There was no way to hide my confusion.

I found out Mrs. Bennington had been talking to Momma the day Momma said, "Your teacher called to tell me you need a little help with your reading, Letty. Is that true?"

"Yes'm."

"Why didn't you say anything about it before now?"

I shrugged.

"Well, we'll make a family project out of getting you caught up."

That was Momma. If there was something that needed fixing, she got everybody into it. She was sure the combined efforts of all the Millers would be enough to teach me how to read.

She was wrong. They all tried to help, but I just couldn't see what they were talking about. How did they get "run, Dick, run" out of the funny black squiggles in the book?

One by one, they gave up on me. Even Lorenzo. After trying to help me for a while, he just threw down the book and walked away. "Stupid. Rubber Brain. Dumbhead. You could do this if you wanted to."

I did want to. I would have fed the cows for a month if Lorenzo had only told me how to read. I would have washed dishes the rest of my life for a hint from Cheryl or Alma. But nobody told me the secret, and no matter how hard I tried, I just couldn't see what they saw. It was like everybody else was looking out at the same world, and I was looking at a world that was all my own.

Finally, it got so bad that Mrs. Bennington sent a note home with me. Momma read it and said, "It looks like I need to talk to your teacher. You don't have to ride the bus home tomorrow night. After I get done talking with her, we can go home together."

When Momma came to the classroom, Mrs. Bennington gave me a puzzle of the United States to work on and sent me to the quiet corner. I guess she thought it would keep me busy, but I had put that puzzle together a thousand times. It was one of my favorites, because I liked the look and feel of the shapes. I could have put the whole puzzle together without looking, so listening to what Mrs. Bennington had to say to Momma didn't slow me down one bit.

"Faye," Mrs. Bennington began, "I'm concerned about Letty and her reading. She shouldn't be having this sort of difficulty. I wouldn't have been surprised at all if it was little Dinah Knotts who was having trouble. You know the Knotts family . . . "

"I know them," said Momma. She didn't much like finding out that even compared to Dinah I wasn't doing well.

"It's different with your daughter," continued Mrs. Bennington. Her voice sounded like she had a clothespin on her nose. "Letty's really very quick. If I explain something to her verbally, she catches right on. But when it comes down to spelling or reading, well . . . "

I was so still, I could scarcely breathe. This was the part I most wanted to hear. Now Mrs. Bennington would tell Momma why, and then she would tell her how. Why I was the way I was, and how I could get over being that way. And then everything would be different. I could start over, and reading would be easy. It would be like taking off my heavy, mud-caked shoes after I'd been walking down the ditch bank, and then running barefoot across the cool lawn.

"When it comes to written work or reading," repeated Mrs. Bennington, "she is very stubborn."

"Stubborn?" Momma repeated in a funny tone.

"I don't know what else it could be. Like I said, she's bright. She is one of the best in the class in math. There's no reason in the world why she can't learn to read."

"Then you think she just has to try harder?"

"Yes, but she also has to *want* to read."

"I do want to read!" I cried. I jumped up from the table so fast that I knocked the United States all over the floor. In a frenzy, I grabbed Mrs. Bennington's arm and shook it. "I do want to read! I do!"

"Letty! Stop that right now!" Momma exclaimed, pulling me away from my teacher and putting her arms around me tight so I couldn't move. "I'm sorry," she said.

"So am I," said Mrs. Bennington.

"I don't know what to do."

"Neither do I."

All the way home, Momma was muttering under her breath. She marched into the house with her mouth grim and her nostrils flaring.

"Well?" questioned Daddy.

"She compared us to the Knotts family!" fumed Momma, and then she proceeded to tell Daddy what had occurred. "I will not have it," she concluded. "You, Miss Lor-etta Miller, are going to learn to read!"

The sessions at the kitchen table grew stormy. Most of the time they ended up with me bawling and Momma telling me to stop being lazy.

"Be tough, kiddo," said Alma one night. That surprised me, because most of the time, he didn't pay any attention to me at all. But that night, he even put his arm around me and squeezed. "She gets like this," he confided, "but it never lasts too long."

I kept hoping he was right, but Momma and I sat at the table night after night. Once, Daddy came in and said, "Faye, is this worth it? You're not getting anywhere."

"I would be if she'd stop being so stubborn about it!"

"I don't really think it's a matter of being stubborn. I think maybe she has the same problem Orvel has."

"Orrin!" Momma said in a voice that meant trouble.

"Anyway, there are other things in life. It doesn't matter if she isn't too good at reading."

"I can't believe I heard you say that."

"All I know is, this can't go on," said Daddy. And I could tell he meant it.

Later on, he put me on his lap and tried to explain what was happening. "If only Mrs. Bennington hadn't said Knotts and Miller in the same breath. It was the absolute worst thing she could have done."

"Why?"

"Because in your momma's mind, there's a world of difference between Knotts and Miller. You see, your momma comes from a very proud family. And they had reason to be proud."

He paused thoughtfully, then asked, "What's your grandpa and grandma's last name?"

"You mean Miller?"

"No. Your other set of grandparents."

"Grandma and Grandpa Pryor."

"Right. And what's the name of our town?"

"Pryor Creek. Why, it's the same!"

Daddy nodded. "Because our town was named after Grandpa Pryor. He was the first mayor. And until he died, he was the most important man around. People look up to us, partly because your momma's a Pryor.

"Now, about the Knotts family. They're newcomers to Pryor Creek. They came up to work in the beets one spring."

"I thought the Mexicans worked the beets," I said.

"Down South, there are some white folks who do field work, too," said Daddy. "The Knottses worked their way north along with the season one year, and they just stayed."

"Oh."

"That's the first reason your momma is in an uproar. She feels like we should be above Asa and Idabelle and their kids. In every way."

"What's the other reason?"

Daddy drew a deep breath. "The other reason has to do with Uncle Orvel. Your Uncle Orvel was . . . a great disappointment to Grandpa Pryor. He had it in mind that Orvel would take over for him, both on the ranch and as a figure of importance in the town. But Orvel was born . . . different.

"Because of your uncle's problems, it was obvious from the beginning that he wouldn't make much of a farmer or rancher. But Grandpa Pryor figured that he could still be a lawyer or businessman. Until they found out that Orvel couldn't read."

"Oh," I said in a small voice.

"It was hard on your grandparents. It was hard on your momma, too. People asked her so often about Orvel's problems that she got to hate it."

"What *is* the matter with him?"

"Well, nobody rightly knows, Letty. But he's managed to make a good life for himself. Orvel Pryor is well respected and loved by everyone who knows him."

"Does Momma still hate it that Uncle Orvel is her brother?"

"No, sweetie. I think she's gotten over that."

I wasn't at all sure that he was right. I took a deep breath before asking, "Do you think she'll get over being ashamed that I'm her little girl?"

Daddy made a funny noise. "I guarantee it," he said in a muffled voice.

CHAPTER FIVE

Somebody told Uncle Orvel that I was having trouble reading. I don't know who it was, but it could have been Daddy, or one of my brothers. Or my sister, Cheryl. It for sure wasn't Momma.

Whoever it was must have told him when they were in town one day, because Uncle Orvel didn't come out to the farm very often. That might have been because he couldn't drive very well. But I don't think so.

Uncle Orvel made cowboy boots and repaired shoes and bridles and such in the back of the Shoe and Saddle Shop. We always took our shoes to him when the seams came loose or the soles wore out. I'll never forget how he looked, hunched over the big sewing machine with a little light shining right down on the shoe he was working on.

He looked scary.

His head was too big and hung out over his chest in a funny way. His back was all humped, too, and his bones stuck out where they shouldn't. Whenever anyone walked into the shop, he'd say, "Good morning. How would you like to be laughed at?"

"Why does he say that?" I once asked Momma.

"That's just his way of saying hello," she answered.

Anyway, if he hadn't been my uncle, I would have been afraid to look at him, like I was afraid to look at the man with the claw instead of a hand. But I'd known Uncle Orvel all my life, and he wasn't scary to me. In fact, he was the nicest of all my relatives. He knew how to tell stories and do magic tricks. And he knew all about not being able to read.

Toward the spring of my first year in school, I rode into town with Daddy. He dropped me off at the Shoe and Saddle Shop while he did the rest of his business.

"Good morning. How would you like to be laughed at?" asked Uncle Orvel.

I grinned. "Howdy."

"Hey, Buck! If anybody comes in, tell 'em I'm busy with a beautiful young lady," Uncle Orvel called to his partner, Buck Wellington. Then he slid off his stool and opened the door to the little apartment he lived in behind the store. "After you," he said, bowing.

I figured he was going to show me a magic trick with a silver dollar or a bandana, but instead, he said, "Hear you're having trouble reading."

I hung my head, but he took my chin in his hand and tipped it up. Because Uncle Orvel was bent and twisted, and because he stopped growing when he was little, he really wasn't much bigger than I was. He looked right into my eyes and didn't let me blink.

"It's okay," he said.

"Oh, but it isn't! Everybody thinks I'm stupid! They think I could do better if I tried harder, but I've tried so hard . . . " The tension that had been building up since school started broke through, and I started to blubber.

"There, there. You go right ahead and cry if you want to."

I leaned right up against him, and he put his arms around me. It was always a surprise how comfortable it was in Uncle Orvel's arms. With all his bones jutting out in the wrong places, you would have thought it wouldn't be, but it was real nice.

"Listen," said Uncle Orvel, "neither one of us is stupid. But there is something . . . Some people are born color-blind, did you know that?"

"What's color-blind?"

"When a person can't see a color. Like red."

"Some people can't see red?"

"Nope. And some are so color-blind that all they see is black and white and gray. Like a photograph."

I closed my eyes and put Uncle Orvel into a black and white picture. Then I put the whole room in the picture, and then the whole house and all my family. "That must be awful," I concluded.

He nodded. "With us, it's like we were born word-blind."

"You mean not everybody sees things the way we do?"

"I don't think so. Just imagine what it must be like for someone who is color-blind to hear people talking about colors—about red and green and blue and gold—and to not know what those words mean."

"You mean some people don't even know when a flower is red? That's dumb."

"Gotcha!" said Uncle Orvel.

At first, I didn't know what I had done. Then it dawned on me. If a person really couldn't see red, he wasn't dumb when he questioned what red was. Dumb had nothing to do with it. It was like not being able to see words.

Uncle Orvel picked up on my thoughts. "You see? It's the same for us. Because most other folks can see the words without any fuss, they can't understand why we can't. And there's no way to tell them."

I remember how Mrs. Bennington reacted when I tried to tell her the letters wouldn't stay still, and I knew Uncle Orvel was right. "Did you ever learn to read real well?" I asked him.

"Oh, I learned to read some and to guess some." He shrugged his hunched shoulders and added, "Reckon I'm a far sight better at guessing than at reading, but I get along okay. The thing is, Letty, you got to keep knowing that you're all right inside, no matter what. And that's going to be tough when everybody's after you to do something you can't."

It was easier said than done. Especially when Mrs. Bennington kept saying things like, "Loretta Miller! If you'd spend as much time trying to learn how to read as you do making up excuses, you'd be the best reader in the class. As it is, you don't read any better than Clyde Robertson."

Clyde Robertson was doing first grade for the second time, and everybody said he would have to do it again because he was so dumb. When Mrs. Bennington compared me to Clyde, I was seized with the fear that I was going to flunk.

Up to now, nobody in our family had ever been held back, but I knew for sure that I, Loretta Miller, was going to be the first. I began to have nightmares that I was in first grade for years and years, till I was real old—at least twelve.

I had to tell Momma what was bothering me the night I woke her up with my screaming. "I'll talk to Mrs. Bennington," she said. Then she held me until I went back to sleep.

The deal Momma and Mrs. Bennington worked out was that if I could learn to write the alphabet, to spell at least ten words, and to read a page out of *Dick and Jane*, I could pass. "She says you're too good at everything else to stay back," Momma explained, "but you do have to show that you're really trying to learn."

I knew what that meant.

It meant more nights around the kitchen table. And things didn't go any better this round than they did before.

"I'm going to flunk," I told Lorenzo as I studied the letters on my pile of wooden blocks. He was trying to teach me to spell with Joe's building blocks.

"I don't think so," he assured me. "Here, let me see what you're doing."

I turned my blocks around. "But I am," I sighed. "At least Dinah will have to stay back with me. She can read better than I can, but she's not so hot at math."

"No she won't." Lorenzo's voice was thick with special knowledge.

"How do you know?"

" 'Cause I heard the principal tell your teacher it wouldn't do any good to hold her back.' "

Tears sprang to my eyes. "I don't believe you."

"It's the truth, scout's honor. I was in the hall when Miss Delmar was talking to Mrs. Bennington."

"What did she say?"

"She said being held back never helped the Knotts boys. She said that all it accomplished was having them in school more years than anybody wanted them to be. She wants them to be passed, no matter what. And that includes Dinah."

I was so stunned I couldn't even croak.

Lorenzo looked at my blocks. "You remembered how to spell *was*. Now try *big*."

"Keep your dumb blocks!" I cried. "I don't want to play anymore." Then I ran upstairs to the bedroom I shared with Cheryl.

The whole last day of first grade I was so worried about flunking that I couldn't eat my lunch or play jacks or draw dresses for my paper dolls. It was the longest day of my life.

Finally, the moment came. Mrs. Bennington started handing out the report cards, beginning at the first of the alphabet. I watched as the kids took their cards in turn and, right off, looked on the back where it said what grade they were supposed to be in the next year. There was always a pause, a moment when I wasn't sure if they had been passed to second grade or not. Then they smiled. Every one of them from A to M, even Dinah. It looked like I was going to be the only one held back.

Then things started to close in. My ears were buzzing and the room looked fuzzy. When Mrs. Bennington called my name, I couldn't see or hear anything anymore. She had to touch me on the shoulder to get my attention. "Your report card, Letty." I took it wordlessly, turned it over, and stared at the back.

I had learned to read at least a little, but that day I couldn't read at all, not even my own name. Nothing on the back of the report card made any sense. The humming in my ears got louder and louder. My nose and eyes tickled the way they do when I'm going to cry. I wanted to run and hide, but I couldn't.

I don't even know how I got out onto the back step of the school building after the last bell rang. Suddenly I found myself standing there, my report card in hand. All around me kids were running and laughing and throwing papers into the air. It was a celebration, but I couldn't celebrate. I went out to the bus and sat down.

"What's the matter, Letty?" It was my sister Cheryl, who had slipped into the seat beside me. Her ponytail bounced when she spoke, and she looked like a cheerleader even though she wasn't wearing her junior high cheerleading outfit.

"Come on, what is it?" Cheryl asked again.

I started to cry. "I . . . I flunked!"

"No you didn't."

"Yes I did!"

"Let me see your report card."

I slowly handed it over. There was no sense in trying to keep it a secret. Soon enough, everybody would know.

"Why do you think you flunked? Didn't you even look at the back of the report card?"

I nodded.

"Then how come . . . " When she remembered how bad I was at reading, she stopped. "You poor kid. You can't read what it says, can you?"

"N-n-no," I sobbed.

She put her arm around me and pulled me close to her. "You don't need to cry. You passed!"

I was so startled that I stopped crying. "I *did?*"

"Yep. Look, it says so right there."

She held out the card and pointed to the most important line. I blinked and looked and blinked again. Then I held my head just so, and there it was.

"Lor-etta Mill-er," I read, sounding out my name.

"Is." That was easy, but I couldn't get the next word.

"Promoted," Cheryl said.

"*To second grade!*" I yelled, not even bothering to read the last words.

It was a celebration after all.

CHAPTER SIX

"Mrs. Bennington passed you because you're so good at math and other things," said Momma. "Also, I promised her that I would work with you every day this summer."

I smiled. I knew how busy Momma was during the summers. She may have thought she would practice reading with me, but I knew she wouldn't have the time. Before me were three whole months of no school and no reading! I couldn't wait to ride with Lorenzo, or play cowboys and Indians around the haystack. Or go target practicing with Lorenzo's BB gun. 'Course, to do that, we'd have to have Alma along. Momma was sure we were going to shoot one another if he wasn't there.

But Lorenzo didn't want to play with me much that summer. He was eleven, and Daddy said that was old enough to start driving the John Deere. Lorenzo thought that was real great. It made him feel like he was a grown-up. When he started driving the tractor for Daddy, he stopped playing with me. Unless Momma or Daddy told him to, and then he grumbled.

Actually, I think he still liked playing cowboys and Indians, and going swimming with me. He just didn't want me to know it.

What with Lorenzo pretending to be grown-up, I didn't have a friend that summer. That's when I started thinking maybe I'd like to see Dinah sometimes. I wasn't sure I liked her that much, but I had gotten used to having her around. Besides, she was the only girl that lived close to us. It would be easy to go visit: all I had to do was ride up the road to her dirt lane on my bike, or walk along the top of the alfalfa field.

"No," said Momma when I asked her.

"Why not?"

"Because they aren't the kind of people we associate with."

"Why? Because they worked the beets once?"

Momma looked at me sharply.

"Who told you that?"

"Daddy. Let me go, Momma. All I want to do is ride bikes with her."

"No. And anyway, I doubt if Dinah Knotts even has a bike."

I tried to talk to Lorenzo about it, but he agreed with Momma. "They're dirty. And every one of them is a re-tard!"

I flew to Dinah's defense. "Dinah is not a re-tard!"

"Well, her brothers are."

"How do you know?"

He shrugged. "Everybody knows."

"That's not fair, Lorenzo!"

"It may not be fair, but it's true," he taunted.

In spite of Momma and Lorenzo, I did get to see Dinah that summer at the swimming hole.

There was only one place to swim in the canal that runs behind all the farms on the bench, and that was by the old wooden bridge where the current isn't so swift. Alma discovered it when he was a kid. Dinah and her brothers knew about it, too, but they usually left if we were already there, or if we came while they were swimming.

That changed one day when Cheryl took Lorenzo, Joe, and me down to the canal. Dinah and Henry had beat us to it; they were already floating downstream on their old inner tube when we got there.

"Looks like we can't swim today," said Lorenzo, real snooty.

Henry pulled the inner tube out of the water and started to leave, but Dinah just stood on the bank, looking at me.

"Hi," I said.

"Hi."

"You done swimming?"

"We just got here."

"Then why are you leaving?"

Dinah looked at Henry, who had stopped to wait for her. His feet were all muddy from walking in the dust without drying them off. "Come on!" he called.

"Cheryl, can't they stay?" I pleaded. "Dinah can share my inner tube."

"It's public property," Cheryl said, sliding into the canal. Then she turned to catch Joe as he jumped.

Dinah grinned.

"Let's go!" I yelled, starting for the grassless slope a ways up the canal. Lorenzo's voice brought me to a skidding stop just as I was about to jump into the water.

"I'm not staying if she does."

I turned around to see Lorenzo glaring at me. His face didn't look very nice. It was all pinched up and dark, and I knew he was telling me to make a choice. I hesitated. Lorenzo was my brother, but I liked Dinah too, and I wanted a friend that was my age.

My eyes swung from Lorenzo to Dinah and back again, then I made up my mind. The way their faces looked did it for me. Lorenzo looked plain mad, but Dinah looked . . . well, she looked on the outside like I feel on the inside sometimes.

"Go home if you want to," I said to Lorenzo. "I'm going swimming."

"Cheryl, make her come home."

Cheryl surprised me. She just shook her head and said, "Tell Momma we'll be home later."

"I'm not telling Momma nothing," Lorenzo grumbled.

After Lorenzo tramped down the road, Henry came back. He didn't do much with me or Dinah, though. Mostly, he kept watching Cheryl like he thought she was going to shoo him off, but she didn't.

Dinah and I had lots of fun riding the current in our inner tubes from the bridge down to the big curve where we had to get out. When it was time to go, I whispered, "We always come after three o'clock. Momma says we won't get sunburned so bad if we wait till then."

Dinah nodded. She understood what I meant.

Lorenzo told on us, like he said he would, but Momma said there wasn't much she could do about who went swimming in the canal.

From then on, I got to swim with Dinah. Lorenzo stomped off the first few times she was there, then he gave up being mad. Swimming was the only way to get cool on those hot, dry afternoons.

I think Momma knew I had fixed it up with Dinah to come at the same time we always came, but she didn't say anything about it. I guess she thought there wasn't much harm in us swimming together, as long as Dinah didn't have any sores.

Like I figured, Momma never did get around to practicing my reading with me that summer. At first, she talked about doing it a lot. "Letty," she would say, "we just have to get at your reading." It didn't happen though. She was too busy.

Then she tried assigning me to the older kids again. They were supposed to take turns working with me, a different one each night. That didn't work either because they had other things they wanted to do. My reading wasn't their problem. After a while, Momma just let it drop.

It seemed like the only person who was worried about my reading was Uncle Orvel. Every time we went into town, I would visit him at the Shoe and Saddle Shop. It was my favorite place to go, because I loved the smell of the new leather. Old leather has a good smell, too, but it's different. It's kind of salty. Well, that new leather smell hit you the moment you opened the door to the shop.

In the middle of the shop stood sawhorses with saddles on them. Some were plain, but not all. The ones I liked had beautiful tooling and shiny silvery conchos. And big, curved horns, and high backs, and tapaderos with points so long they touched the floor.

On one wall hung bridles with all kinds of bits and long reins. There were hackamores, too, and halters. I loved the way Buck had lined them all up like they were decorations.

There weren't really shoes in the Shoe and Saddle Shop. There were boots: regular boots, fancy boots with different colors of leather on the tops, even boots with embroidery. Daddy didn't have boots like that. Neither of the boys did, either. They weren't the kind of boots a man worked in. The only time I saw boots like that on anybody's feet was at the Fourth of July parade. Then fancy boots and saddles like the ones in the shop were everywhere.

What I liked most about going to the Shoe and Saddle Shop was that Buck didn't mind if I touched any of the things he had on display. Sometimes he would even let me sit on one of the big saddles. Buck looked like a fence post, he was so tall and thin. His face was brown, and his teeth were brown too. From chewing tobacco, my momma said.

He always had a wad in his cheek and every so often he would spit into a coffee can behind the counter.

Anyway, it was the same every time I came to visit that summer. Buck would say, "How do, young lady," and spit in the coffee can. And Uncle Orvel would say, "Good morning. How would you like to be laughed at?" Then, after I'd talked to them both a bit, Uncle Orvel would ask me, "How's your reading coming?" I would shrug my shoulders and say, "Okay."

I guess he got tired of hearing that, because one day he stopped what he was doing and looked right at me. "Letty, are you practicing at all?"

"No, sir. Nobody has time to help me."

"You tell your mother to come see me before you go home, okay?"

I nodded.

At first, Momma didn't like Uncle Orvel's suggestion that she bring me in for lessons three times a week. "I don't see how it will work," she told Daddy. "He has almost as much trouble reading as she does."

"Maybe. But who else has the time or inclination to help her?"

Momma flew off the handle. "Orrin Miller! You know I'd help her if I weren't so busy canning and sewing!"

"Whoa," said Daddy, holding up his hand. "Hold up a bit. I'm not saying you're neglecting Letty. I'm just saying none of us ever gets around to it. If Orvel wants to help, let him help."

We decided I should go in three times a week at noon. Every day, when the noon whistle at the sugar factory blew, Buck would close the shop and go home for lunch. Uncle Orvel would have lunch in his little apartment. I was to join Uncle Orvel at his kitchen table for my lessons during that time.

Well, for the first time, reading lessons were fun. Uncle Orvel wasn't in a big hurry. He didn't seem to care if I couldn't figure something out right off. We just kept trying to find a way of looking at it that would work.

One of the things that worked was when I used my finger to trace letters over and over again. That's what gave Uncle Orvel the idea of letting me use his wood burner to make dark letters on leftover scraps of leather from one of his projects. He used the wood burner to make part of his designs darker than the rest.

"Hold it like this," he instructed me. "And be careful that you don't burn yourself with it. It's awful hot."

Other times, he gave me one of his modeling tools, so I could trace and then deepen the lines of a letter into the smooth leather.

"Why don't we do your name?" he asked one day. He used a sharp knife to cut out a nice rectangular piece of leather. Then he dampened it down and used a stencil to trace my name in the middle of it.

The letters he traced weren't plain, like the ones I had been doing. They were nice and wide, and they had little curlicues on the tops and bottoms. After he traced them, Uncle Orvel handed me a modeling tool. It was like a smooth stick with metal points on each end.

"This is a deer-foot," he said. "You're going to use it to deepen the lines."

My hand was shaking a little bit as I took the deer-foot in hand. At home, I never got to do much, because I was too little to do it right. I was terrified that I would make a mistake, and then Uncle Orvel wouldn't let me do any more. Every time I went outside the line, I made a moan of distress.

"It's okay," Uncle Orvel kept assuring me. "It'll turn out all right. After all, this is just your first try."

We only did a little bit every time I came in, so it was a week before I had finished making all the lines deeper. Then Uncle Orvel said, "Now, we're going to make them stand out."

"How are we going to do that?"

"By stamping down the leather around each letter. Here, I'll show you." He positioned a little metal stamp right up against the line of my L, and hit it with a leather hammer. When he took away the stamp, the leather in that spot was pressed flat.

"Now you try."

Working together, Uncle Orvel and I stamped down the leather all around the L that day. I couldn't believe my eyes when I saw what that did. The L stood out right proud like. I kept running my finger over it from top to bottom.

"Let's do a P next," I said excitedly. Uncle Orvel was mystified, but he got another piece of scrap leather, and we did a P.

I don't know why it made a difference, but when I traced a letter, deepened the lines, and then stamped down the leather around it, I really saw it. Same for when I drew a letter with the wood-burning tool. Or if I darkened a fancy letter with it.

Discovering that B's and P's didn't turn around or float when I burned them into scrap leather was the most exciting thing that had ever happened to me. After that, when Uncle Orvel held up an alphabet card, I would move my eyes down the lines just as if I were burning them into a piece of leather.

My new technique worked. It took most of what was left of summer, but I finally got so if I concentrated hard enough, I could make all the letters hold still.

When I could recognize most of them, most of the time, Uncle Orvel said, "Time to start on words." At first, I used my old tricks to figure out what the words were, but Uncle Orvel wasn't fooled. He knew what I was doing.

"Letty, it won't work. Maybe it does now, but it won't in the long run."

In the long run. In the long run. I mouthed the words and tried to imagine what they meant. Before I had it figured out, Uncle Orvel said, "Let's get to work."

It didn't seem like work to me. Tooling leather or learning words with Uncle Orvel was as much fun as swimming and target practicing. I got pretty good at following the letters Uncle Orvel traced on the leather, and I knew which tools made a fat line and which made a thin line and which stamps I liked the best. Lots of times, I was still working at Uncle Orvel's bench when Buck came back at one o'clock.

I was having such a good time, I wanted summer to go on forever. And then, suddenly, it was over. All it took was Momma saying, "Gracious, we'd better get you all some new shoes before school starts!"

The next day, Momma drove us into town and parked in front of a new store. The display window was filled with nothing but shoes, the most beautiful shoes I had ever seen. Shoes with high heels and low heels, shoes with fancy buckles. Shoes that were shiny; shoes that were suede. I knew just by looking at them how they would feel when I ran my fingers over them, and how they would smell if I put my nose up close.

But Momma bought me saddle shoes.

"They're sturdy," Momma said when I asked her why.

"But they're ugly!" I complained.

"Shoes don't have to be pretty, they have to be serviceable."

I didn't know what *serviceable* meant, but I knew better than to argue. Still, it was an awful waste.

CHAPTER SEVEN

In a way, starting a new school year was a lot like New Year's Day: everything was different, but in a strange way, everything was the same.

That year, I walked into the classroom on the opposite side of the hall from Mrs. Bennington's room. The windows faced south instead of north, and the teacher's desk was at the wrong end, but the tables and chairs were exactly the same size as the ones we'd had in first grade. I guess they thought we wouldn't grow enough in one summer to need bigger chairs and tables.

The second-grade teacher was Mrs. Norton. When I first saw her, I thought she looked more like a grandmother than a teacher. She talked like a teacher, though. The first thing she did was assign seats.

"Knotts, Dinah. You sit here, dear. And Letty Miller, your seat is next to Dinah's."

As if I didn't know.

This part is true, I swear: Dinah was wearing the exact same dress that she wore the first day of first grade. Only it was dirtier.

"Now class. I want you to get out your paper."

I had a new, red Big Chief tablet and some yellow pencils that I had already sharpened to a point. I got them out.

"Across the top write what I have already put on the board. Who will read it for us? Gloria?"

Gloria Nesbitt read, "One Thing I Did This Summer."

"That's right. After you've copied that title, think of one special thing you did and write a few lines about it. If you need help with spelling, just ask me."

I looked at the blackboard real hard and did all the tricks Uncle Orvel had taught me. And guess what! I could read what was written there. 'Course, it helped knowing what it said beforehand.

Thinking about Uncle Orvel was what gave me the idea to write all about the Shoe and Saddle Shop and Buck Wellington.

I had to have a lot of help. Knowing how to read a little is not the same as knowing how to spell. Some words I figured out on my own, some I asked Dinah how to spell. The ones she didn't know, I asked Mrs. Norton about. Every few minutes I raised my hand to get her attention.

"Yes, Letty?"

"How do you spell *shop?*"

"Yes, Letty?"

"How do you spell *interesting?*"

When I asked her how to spell *tobacco*, she looked at me funny. And when I asked her how to spell *swear*, she said, "Letty Miller, let me see what you're writing."

"Wait till I get done, please?" I begged. I felt real proud as I held out my paper to her. I had written:

One Thing I Did This Summer
One thing I did this summer was go to the shu and saddle shop I met mr bk He ons the stor He is very interesting He cues tobacco and spts in a kofe kan he is a veri good spitr He can swear rel good to he swears betr than enibodi i no

48

"My goodness, Letty! Is that all you could think of to write about?" Mrs. Norton asked.

"What's wrong with it?"

"It's not appropriate."

I had heard that word a lot at home. I knew what the meaning of *appropriate* was. It was what adults want kids to do. And there was no arguing with it. With Mrs. Norton's help, I wrote another paper about going fishing up the mountain.

And then, Mrs. Norton had each of us read one page. I was anxious to read because I wanted to show how much Uncle Orvel had helped me during the summer. Dinah was real impressed. "Wow! You can read!" she said, right out loud.

I grinned.

But Mrs. Norton wasn't impressed. When she divided up the class into reading groups, she put me in the bottom group—me and Clyde Robertson. Dinah was in the group ahead of us.

When Momma found that out, she had a fit. "See, Orrin! I told you it wouldn't work out having Orvel help her. It's the blind leading the blind."

Then the sessions around the kitchen table started all over again.

See what I mean about things not changing?

CHAPTER EIGHT

The summer between second and third grade, I kept
bugging Momma to let me go over to Dinah's.

"What is this about going to Dinah's? Why do you per-
sist in asking me?" demanded Momma finally.

"I'm lonesome," I said.

It was the truth. Although I didn't really *like* Dinah
Knotts, I was lonesome without her. She had been right at
my shoulder all through second grade, protecting me and
prompting me. Not having her with me seemed like suddenly having my shadow disappear, even though the sun
was still shining.

I asked Momma so many times that she finally decided
the best way to cure me of wanting to go over to Dinah's
was to let me go.

I was excited when I started down the lane, but when I
got close to the Knotts house, my excitement changed to
fear. It looked rattier than it had from the bus, and I could
see things I never noticed when Lorenzo and I rode down
the lane to go over the big bump.

There were lots of rusted cans lying by the side of the
road, and the wind had blown papers and trash into a pile
at the base of some of the sagebrush. There was a gully not
too far from the lane, and somebody had thrown an old
refrigerator and some bedsprings down into it.

That didn't bother me too much. People who lived in the country tossed their trash wherever they wanted to. Daddy even once drove a pickup full of junk out in the hills behind our place and dumped it. But the dead calf lying by the side of the road nearly made me turn around.

It was half-hidden by a willow clump, that's why I'd never seen it from the bus. It had been dead a long time, 'cause it didn't stink. Underneath what was left of the skin there was nothing but bones, and the eye sockets were clean and dry.

"Hi, Letty."

It was Dinah. She had come out of the house while I was looking at the calf. She was wearing a T-shirt and pair of pants that had holes in both knees. The pants were too big for her. The only thing that kept them up was the bailing twine she had threaded through the loops and tied in a knot in front. She was barefoot.

"You can get sick if you don't wear shoes," I said.

"I can?" she asked, looking down at her feet.

"Yep. My momma never lets me go barefoot, except sometimes if I promise to stay on the grass. She says my jaw will freeze and I'll starve to death if I step on a nail or anything rusty, and I'll end up with worms inside if I step in a cow pie when I have a cut."

Dinah's feet shifted uncertainly. "We hafta save our shoes," she explained.

I remembered how her saddle shoes looked and wished I hadn't said anything. To change the subject, I said, "Did that cat of yours have its kittens yet?"

"Yeah. Do you want to see it?"

I nodded. Dinah led me to a haystack that looked as if it would fall over any minute. It was old hay, and moldy. Bales lay broken open and half-used around the stack, and the ground was covered with circles of twine, something my daddy would never have allowed. In a space between

51

two of the bottom bales was the momma cat and her one kitten, a tiger stripe.

"Oh, she's cute!" I cried. "Can I hold her?"

Dinah carefully reached in and brought the little kitten out into the light. I held it to my shoulder and petted it. Its little paws opened and closed, pricking my skin beneath my shirt as it nuzzled.

"Is this the only one? Our cat had seven the last time."

"We had lots more, but my pa drowned them in the canal."

"Oh." Dinah's matter-of-factness gave me shivers.

"What does your pa do with all your kittens?"

I shook my head dumbly. For the first time, I realized the number of cats we had around the place didn't match up with the number of kittens produced every year. I wondered what happened to them. But I wasn't sure I wanted to know.

We played with the kitten for a while, then played cowboys. I was the Lone Ranger and Dinah was Tonto. We fought off bad Indians from behind the chicken coop and galloped our pretend horses up and down the draw. While we were playing Bob and Henry came home. They were carrying a bunch of dead magpies.

"How many did you get?" cried Dinah, running up the draw to see their booty.

"Ten!"

"Ohhh," Dinah said, clearly impressed.

"We almost got a bobcat, too," said Henry. "If we had'a, we'd have enough money to go to the movies every Saturday for a year!"

"If you go to the movies so much, how come I never see you?" I asked.

"Which show house do you go to?" asked Dinah.

"The Marlow Theater."

"That's why," she said. "We go to the other one."

The Rainbow Theater was off-limits for Millers. For one thing, it was in a real old building made of adobe, and my momma was afraid it would catch fire when we were in there. The other reason was the kind of movies they showed. They were all horror movies, with Boris Karloff and Bela Lugosi.

Momma didn't know it, but Lorenzo and I went to the Rainbow Theater once. She had given each of us a quarter to go the show that day. Well, a ticket to the Marlow Theater cost the whole quarter, but a ticket to the Rainbow cost only a dime. We decided to go to the Rainbow and spend the difference on candy and popcorn.

We only went once, because I got too scared. There had been a scene in the movie we saw where the hero and the heroine were in a prison cell that had metal walls, and the walls started to heat up and move in. I thought for sure the hero and heroine were going to get cooked or squished. I grabbed onto Lorenzo's arm and squeezed so hard that he yelped. Afterward, he showed me the marks my fingernails had made.

Lorenzo probably went to the Rainbow Theater again, but never with me.

"Do you like horror shows?" I asked Dinah.

"Sure!" she exlaimed. As we walked toward the house, she started to tell me all about the latest movie she'd seen. By the time she was finished, I had been at her house way over an hour, which was as long as Momma had said I could stay.

"Guess I ought to go home," I said.

Dinah hesitated, then she said, "I made a cake. Do you want a piece?"

I looked doubtfully at the house. The inside was probably in worse shape than the outside, I knew, and I really didn't want to eat anything Dinah had made. But her eyes had a look in them that I understood, so I said yes.

The Knotts house was of unpainted wood. There was no grass or trees around it to make it look better: it sat in the dirt all by itself. The screen door was darker in the middle from unwashed hands opening it, and the screen was torn loose and curled up in one corner. As I followed Dinah through the door, my heart began pounding.

I was right. It didn't look any better on the inside than it did on the outside. The table where Dinah told me to sit was not even, in spite of the fact that some comic books had been piled up under one of the legs. The top was covered with an odd assortment of chipped and cracked dishes, the kind I'd seen out where people dump things. They had bits of dried, funny-colored food on them. It was all I could do to keep from upchucking right then.

Dinah had made a chocolate cake. She cut a piece for me with a knife she wiped clean on her T-shirt. Then she put the cake on a plate. "We don't have any milk to go with it, but I can get you some water," she said as she handed me the plate.

"Okay," was all I could trust myself to say.

"I have to go out to the cistern to get it. The well is nasty." She pulled a face. "Smells like rotten eggs. We wash the dishes in it, but we don't drink it."

The screen door slammed shut behind her, and I sat there looking at the cake. I picked the plate up and smelled it. It looked mighty funny, but it smelled good. I might have eaten it if the piles of dirty plates and the junk on the floor hadn't ruined my appetite. Besides, I could remember Momma saying, "I'd rather die than eat anything prepared by Idabelle Knotts."

I can't eat it! I thought, but I didn't want to make Dinah feel bad. I decided to hide it and then pretend that I had eaten it.

I looked around the room for a trash can. There was trash everywhere, but no can. Then I heard a whimper. An old liver-colored dog was standing at the screen door, wagging his tail. Out the side window, I could see Dinah on her way back from the cistern. Quickly, I shoved the cake through the torn screen. The dog gulped it down in two bites and licked up the telltale crumbs.

When Dinah came back in, I was sitting at the table, pretending to chew. I swallowed and said, "That was great cake."

"Do you want another piece?" she asked.

"No, thanks. My momma doesn't like me to eat too many sweets. I've got to get going, now. I don't want her to get mad at me."

"Here's your water."

I shook my head. "I'm not thirsty."

Riding back down the lane, up the road, and then into our own farmyard was like coming out of a horror movie back into the sunlight. Momma would never have to tell me I couldn't go to Dinah's again, because I didn't want to—ever. It was too awful. And it made me feel too bad.

CHAPTER NINE

After my visit to the Rock Pile, there was only one thing on my mind: rescuing Dinah.

I had thought—because of my one venture into the Rainbow Theater—that I knew what terror was. I had felt it twice, once during the movie itself and once during the dream I'd had about it the same night. But that feeling was nothing compared to the terror I felt when I dreamed I was a prisoner on the Rock Pile.

In my dream, I was Dinah. I was standing in the middle of that dreadful, filthy kitchen. *Peeyew!* I thought. *I'm not going to stay here.* I didn't have any idea what was going to happen as I walked over to the door and tried to open it.

At first, I thought it was stuck. I turned the knob again and pushed against the door with my shoulder. It didn't move. I turned the knob harder, ramming with my shoulder at the same time. "Hey, somebody open this dumb door!" I called.

Nobody answered.

I looked around me. The corners of the room were gathering shadows and the chairs standing in the middle of the trash looked like animals crouching in the grass.

Fear began creeping up inside me. "Let me out! Somebody let me out. Please!" I cried. I began pounding and kicking at the door, but the door got stronger with every

56

blow. And then it turned to stone. Looking from the stone door to my bloodied hands, I knew I was a prisoner in the house.

My gaze flew around the room in desperation. *The window!* I thought. Surely I could smash a window! I flung myself against the nearest pane of glass, fists flailing.

They might as well have been moth wings.

And then in my dream, I was a moth, beating my wings to shreds against the windowpane.

I woke up sweating, my mouth open for the scream that was pushing its way up. It never came out; it stopped in my throat when I realized that I was my own self, in my own bed.

The sound of Cheryl's steady breathing came from the bed next to mine. I was saved! With a muffled sob, I lay back down and cried silent tears of relief.

That was when I promised myself that I would get Dinah Knotts off the Rock Pile—one way or another. It was like buying insurance, I guess. I figured that if she wasn't there, I wouldn't have the dream again. The fact that the next few days went by without a recurrence of the dream didn't change my mind. I wasn't about to take any chances.

So I spent the rest of the summer trying to figure out how to rescue Dinah, but none of my ideas were any good. I figured what Dinah needed was a fairy godmother. It turned out that all she needed was Momma. Momma was the one who finally came up with a plan, and she didn't even realize what she was doing.

It happened when Alma got his mission call to France.

"Why are you going?" I asked him during dinner one evening.

"Because there aren't many places in the world like Pryor Creek," said Alma. "Most places, Mormons would be in a minority."

"What's a minority?"

Alma pursed his lips. "That's hard to explain. Let's see. Is there anybody in your class who isn't a Mormon?"

"Billy Bucher isn't."

"Yes he is," said Lorenzo. "He just goes to another ward."

"Why?"

"Because there's too many Mormons in Pryor Creek to put them all in one ward."

"Oh. What about Gloria Nesbitt?"

"Nesbitts are too, honey," said Daddy. "They live on the other side of town, so they go to the other ward."

I was stumped for a minute. Then I thought of Dinah. She lived right next to us, and she didn't go to our church. "The Knotts!" I said triumphantly.

"Right," agreed Alma. "So they're in the minority."

I was astonished at the implication of what Alma was saying. "You mean there are places in the world where everybody isn't a Mormon?"

"You got it."

"Then what are they?"

All the big kids laughed, and Joe laughed because the big ones did. Momma and Daddy smiled.

"Well, son," said Daddy, putting a toothpick in his mouth, "go ahead and explain it to her."

Alma tried, but all that stuff about Methodists and Baptists and Catholics just mixed me up more.

"And you're going to try to get them to be Mormons?"

"Yep."

"Why?"

Maybe I shouldn't have asked that, but I really didn't know why.

"Because there is only one true church, Letty, and it's the Mormon church. It's our obligation to tell all the people in the world about it."

I thought for a moment, then said, "Then why haven't you told the Knotts family?"

There was a stunned silence.

"Well!" said Momma.

"Can you imagine Bob passing the sacrament?" howled Cheryl.

"What about Henry?" asked Lorenzo. "He's got ring-worm again. I bet nobody would take the sacrament if he was passing it."

"Children! I won't have you talking about them in that manner," scolded Momma.

"You do," I said. "I've heard you."

"Lor-etta Miller, whatever do you mean?"

"You know. 'How can those people *live* like that? Somebody ought to do something about it.'"

Momma blushed, and her eyes had that wide-open look that meant she was ready to blow up.

Daddy just leaned back in his chair and sucked on his toothpick for a long time. Then he shoved it to the corner of his mouth, and said, "Seems we have a problem. Here we are, planning to send Alma off to preach the gospel when we need a good dose of it right here in our own home. We haven't done well by our neighbors, Faye."

"What do you suggest, having them over for dinner?"

"That might be a good start."

I stared at Daddy. Even I knew Momma would rather die than have the Knotts family set foot in our house.

"You can't be serious," she cried.

"I am."

Momma stood up from the table. "I'll talk to you later," she said to Daddy. Then she favored me with one of those looks that meant I was in trouble again.

Momma never did take the time to discipline me, though, because she had too many other things to worry about. What with Alma going to France soon and school about to start, she had a long list of things we had to shop for.

Getting my school shoes always gave me a funny feeling. It was the one thing that said, "Summer's over." That's when I would start to feel anxious and sick, like something was going to happen, and I didn't know what.

I watched Alma trying on shoes, pretty black shoes with a shine Momma would appreciate, and I wondered if he felt kind of sick, too. He wasn't just going back to school, he was going across the ocean to a different country. Lots of evenings he and his girlfriend, Connie, would sit on the bench out in the apple orchard, and most of the time, she was crying. That was funny. Alma was my own brother, but I didn't feel like crying. Still, I wanted to know if he was scared.

I started going out to the barn when he was milking, trying to work up enough courage to ask. It took me a long time, because I was little and Alma was grown up. He had been grown up all the time I could remember. Asking him a question wasn't the same as asking Lorenzo. Lorenzo was used to me and my questions.

Strangely enough, it was Alma who brought up the subject of being scared.

"You're almost eight, aren't you?" he asked me one night.

"My birthday's July 11th," I said.

"That means you'll be getting baptized."

I nodded. My Sunday School teacher had been talking a lot about that lately.

"Are you excited about it?"

"Uh . . . I don't know."

"Maybe a little scared?"

"A little."

"There's nothing to be scared about. Here, I'll show you how it's done."

Right there in the barn, Alma showed me how to position my hand so I could plug my nose when I went under the water. "See, whoever baptizes you will have his hand supporting your back, so you won't feel like you're falling."

Then he went back to milking the cow.

"Want a squirt?"

I squatted down and opened my mouth. He squirted some warm milk right into it.

"You can aim good," I said.

He nodded and went on milking. The streams hit the frothy milk already in the bucket with a rhythmical swoosh. He had asked me if I was scared about getting baptized, so maybe now was the time to ask him if going on a mission made his stomach upset.

"Are *you* scared? About going on a mission, I mean?"

At first I thought he didn't hear me, then I thought he just wasn't going to answer. But when he stopped milking and sighed, I knew he would.

"Yep, but don't tell on me."

"I wouldn't do that!"

He leaned his head on the cow's reddish flank. "I don't know why I'm scared, I've wanted to go on a mission for a long time, now."

"Why?"

"There you go again, asking why. Same thing Connie asks. She'd just as soon we got married."

"Do you want to get married?"

He laughed. "To tell the truth, kiddo, that scares me, too."

"Really? I thought I was the only one who got scared about things."

"What are you scared of—besides getting baptized?"

"Going back to school."

Alma turned on his milking stool (it wasn't really a stool, it was just two boards nailed together to form a *T*) and sat me on his leg. "Here we are, a couple of scaredy-cats. What do you think we should do about it?"

"I don't know."

"Bet you do."

"I know what *you* can do, but not me."

"And what's that?"

"You can just decide not to go."

"Then what would I do with my new blue suit?"

"Get married in it."

"Letty, I really do want to go, even if I am scared."

"Why?" I asked again.

"Have they ever talked to you in your Sunday School class about the Holy Ghost?"

"Yeah."

"Well, I feel the Spirit right here." He touched the pocket of his shirt. "It's the Holy Ghost telling me that I've made the right decision."

"How does he tell you?"

"By the feeling I have."

"What's it like?"

"That's a tough one. You know when we go up the mountain to camp? We build a nice cook fire, one that burns slow and steady and warm. That's what it feels like."

I could understand that. A good cook fire is comfortable to sit by. It doesn't turn your face red, and it doesn't burn the sliced potatoes. "That sounds nice," I said.

"You know, you'll get the gift of the Holy Ghost when you get confirmed."

"What does that mean?"

"Means he'll always be with you."

"Do you have that feeling all the time?"

"No. And you won't either. But when you do, it'll help you know what's right and that God loves you."

"Would he help me learn how to read?"

Alma hugged me. "I don't know, kiddo. But he can help you get through the tough times, even if you never learn how to read very well."

"And I get the Holy Ghost after I get baptized, when I'm confirmed?"

"Yep."

"I think I need him. Can you baptize me?"

"Would you like me to?"

I nodded.

"Then I will."

Alma baptized me in the font of the new church. I don't know how to explain what happened. It was pretty scary, but pretty dull at the same time. I was scared about getting dunked under the water, but Alma said, "You'll be okay. I won't drown you." That made me wonder if anybody ever did get drowned when all they wanted was to get baptized.

It turned out okay, though. The whole family stood around the font while Alma and I walked down the stairs into the water. Alma positioned my hands the way he told me he would and said the words in a voice I'd never heard him use before, not even when he blessed the sacrament. Then he dunked me.

Momma helped me get dressed, then Daddy put his hands on my head and said the words that confirmed me a member of the Church and gave me the gift of the Holy Ghost.

And I didn't feel a thing.

That's what I meant when I said it was pretty dull. I thought I would get that warm feeling right away, but nothing happened. Daddy shook hands with me and Momma hugged me and we went home to dinner, and that was that.

Toward the end of August, Momma and Daddy left the rest of us at home and drove Alma down to Salt Lake. They came back and began talking about wanting to go on a mission themselves. Not too long after that they got called as stake missionaries. That meant they didn't have to leave home. They would only have to find the *minorities,* the ones who weren't Mormons, and tell them about the Church.

Right away, while she was still excited about it, Momma decided to visit Dinah's momma and daddy. "You know how the gospel can change the lives of people who are baptized," she said. "And if there's anybody who needs it, it's the Knotts family."

That was the answer to getting Dinah off the Rock Pile!

I couldn't say for sure that being baptized had changed my life, but I had been in the Knotts house.

I had seen Henry and Bob with magpie legs in their hands, their only way of getting enough money to go to the show. I had looked at Dinah's bare feet and into her eyes that always looked hungry.

And I hoped Momma was right.

CHAPTER TEN

A couple of days before school started, we got a letter from Alma. It was a long letter, full of descriptions of strange things. Some of it confused me, but I understood one thing for sure: France was nothing like Pryor Creek.

At the end of his letter, Alma wrote something specially for me. He wrote: "Hey, kiddo! I didn't really understand what it was like for you, not being able to read. I do now, let me tell you! Everything I hear sounds like gibberish, and all the words look like chicken scratch. But I'm going to figure it out, and you can, too."

I wasn't sure he was right about that, but it made me feel good, anyway.

I felt good right up until the first day of school when Lorenzo announced he wasn't going to catch the bus on the way out anymore.

"Going over the bump is for little kids, not seventh graders."

"Then I'll stop, too," I decided. And I would have, if it hadn't been for Joe. Joe was finally old enough to go to school, and he wanted to see what the bump was like. I didn't blame him. I had felt exactly the same way. What I didn't like was having to ride out to the end of the line without Lorenzo.

"Do I have to?" I asked Momma.

"I don't want him standing out by the road alone," said Momma, wiping her eyes. She had just finished taking our picture. It was the first school picture without Alma and the first one with Joe, and she was real weepy about it.

"But Lorenzo and I are too big to care about the bump anymore!" I protested.

"Lor-etta Miller. You will catch the bus on the way out, with Joe. That's all there is to it."

I was fuming as I stomped out the gate, Joe trailing behind me. I had been trying to catch up with Lorenzo for years and having to take care of Joe always pulled me back. I was more Joe's age than Lorenzo's, but Lorenzo was the one I wanted to be with. Getting on the bus without him was weird.

Worse still, when Lorenzo did get on the bus on the way back into town, he sat up front, leaving me in the back with Joe. And right then, I knew this year was going to be different.

I had no idea just how different it was going to be until Melanie Watts came into my life. My third-grade class had just started writing "What I Did This Summer" across the top of our papers when someone knocked at the door. Mrs. Morehead opened it, and there stood the principal with a girl I had never seen before.

Momma says it's not polite to stare, but I stared. I couldn't help it. I had never seen anyone who looked like she did. She had white skin and blue eyes and red hair that hung down in ringlets past her shoulders. In her hair was a blue ribbon that matched her dress. She had on lace-trimmed anklets and black patent leather shoes. She looked like Easter, and here it was only the first day of school.

"Class, this is Melanie Watts," said Miss Delmar, the principal. "Melanie and her family have just moved into Pryor Creek. Her father is taking over as head of the Forest

Service. Melanie, this is Mrs. Morehead, our third-grade teacher."

Mrs. Morehead smiled at the new girl and drew her into the room with eager delight. "Now you just wait right here a minute, while I figure out where you'll sit."

Melanie smiled at Mrs. Morehead. Then she gazed at us with her steady, extraordinarily blue eyes. Even though all of us were staring at her, she wasn't embarrassed or shy. Her gaze moved over us slowly. When she got to me, I felt the power of that simple act. She was in charge; she expected us to grant her our loyalty and obedience.

All through first and second grade, us kids had been like a herd of sheep wanting a leader. We had wandered in the same direction by common consent; no one of us had taken charge. Melanie Watts changed all that as she stood in front of the class that morning. She became, in less than five minutes, the delight of Mrs. Morehead and the desire and envy of every kid in third grade.

From that time on, Melanie was the one who got to hand out papers, fetch supplies, and choose what book Mrs. Morehead would read from when we had our milk break. During recess, she picked out which games the rest of us were going to play. And each day, she chose the kids she would give her favor to.

Her circle of friends changed from day to day, and it was impossible to tell why we were in it one day and not the next. Those of us that were out on any given day would sometimes play with each other. Most of the time, though, we just floated like weed seeds in the air, attaching ourselves to whatever group presented a surface we could grab onto—all the while waiting for her call. Life as part of Queen Melanie's court was pretty miserable, but we always came at the sound of her voice.

Now that I think about, it was dumb, because Melanie wasn't so hot in anything except pleasing adults. Even Dinah was smarter. We found that out right off when Mrs. Morehead passed out our reading books and told us we would each have a chance to read aloud. And, naturally, she asked Queen Melanie to read first. (So much for alphabetical order.)

Well, Melanie blew it. She stood there all fancy and frilly and smiled her best smile, and she couldn't read worth spit.

It was wonderful.

What happened was this: Because Mrs. Morehead didn't want to be hard on Melanie, she wasn't hard on anybody. "Now, dear, don't you think you can do better?" was her favorite phrase. Maybe it wasn't all just Melanie Mush; she might have been that way anyhow. Either way, it was all right with me. I sure wasn't going to complain.

What with the teacher being so nice and all, it was actually fun to be in reading that year. She thought anything I did was wonderful. 'Course, most of the time, I was pulling the wool over her eyes. I had learned a lot of tricks since I started school, and I could fool just about anybody when it came to reading—except Momma and Uncle Orvel.

Mrs. Morehead didn't catch on. Or if she did, it didn't matter to her. So, on one side of the fence, Melanie's presence in class made my third grade easier, almost pleasant. If it hadn't been for the fact that she was a snoot and a snot, I might have even learned to like her. But on the other side, almost every day, she pulled something that made me wish I could get back at her.

Like the day she decided we should play a game of tag. Not regular tag—this game was different. All of the players were girls, except for the one who was "it." Only a boy could be "it." Rather, only a boy that Queen Melanie *liked* could be "it." The trick was to get to the school step before he could catch us. Any girl who got caught had to let him kiss her.

The first round, Melanie let Billy Bucher be "it." Billy was one of those kids whose hair always looked combed and whose shirttail was never out. No wonder she picked him. I bet she couldn't wait to kiss him.

But I was the first one Billy Bucher caught and kissed. It wasn't very exciting. I mean, how could two pairs of prissed-up lips mashing together be exciting? But being the center of attention for even a few moments was exciting. So when we played the next round, I made sure I got caught again, this time by Stevie McClenahan.

I didn't mind being kissed by Stevie. Not one bit. Things were looking up until Melanie accused me of letting myself get caught on purpose.

"You got caught both times, too," I countered. "Are you letting them catch you on purpose?"

"It doesn't matter. You're out."

Queen Melanie had spoken. I shrugged and walked away from the steps.

There was one place I always went when I wanted to be alone: the corner of the elementary school building. It was an "inny" corner, like an "inny" belly button. I could press my back right up into the corner and then slide down into a squat with my arms around my knees.

I went to that corner, slid down on my heels, and put my head down on my knees. After a while, I felt someone beside me. I looked up and saw Dinah. She was sitting on her heels with her arms around her knees, too. I remembered what Melanie had said at the beginning of recess: "You can't play, Dinah. Who would kiss you?" So there the two of us were, our chins resting on our knees, balancing on our saddle-shoed feet.

It was while we were sitting there that Dinah came up with her name for Queen Melanie.

"Old Wattsie Pottsie thinks she's really something, doesn't she?"

"Old Wattsie Pottsie!" I squealed.

"Shhh. Don't say that out loud! She'll kill us!"

"Old Wattsie Pottsie!" I giggled.

"Actually, she looks like Goldilocks to me. Acts like Goldilocks. Only a Wattsie Pottsie person would go right into somebody else's house without knocking and eat up all the porridge and break all the chairs."

"Too bad we're not doing Goldilocks for the open house. We could change the ending and have the bears eat her up."

"And we could have Clyde Robertson be one of the bears!"

We looked at each other and laughed. Right then, I thought Dinah looked a lot nicer than Wattsie Pottsie, even if her hair looked like she hadn't washed it in six months. And her saddle shoes . . .

I didn't know where Dinah got her saddle shoes, but I guessed somebody had given her their old ones. At least, the ones she had on weren't new, and they didn't fit her very well. They were so big that her heels kept slipping out of them. Half of the time, she walked with her heels out and smashing down the backs, so that finally, the backs never straightened up. Not even when her feet were inside like they were supposed to be.

Well, those shoes bothered me. I don't know why, but I was always looking at them. Especially when we jumped rope.

Dinah was a whiz at jumping rope, even though her shoes slipped half off her feet every time she left the ground. Melanie usually ignored Dinah, but whenever she decided to jump rope, she always let Dinah jump, too.

Red Hot Pepper or One Potato, Two Potato, I can still remember the cadence of the chants and the slap of the rope against the cement of the sidewalk leading to the back steps of the school. And I remember Dinah, jumping and jumping—seventy-eight, seventy-nine, eighty, eighty-one . . .

Most of the time, she could get way up there, unless on Melanie's sign, one of the girls turning the rope pulled it flat so it would land on Dinah's shoulder instead of going over her head. Then Melanie would say, "Oh, you are so good! But now it's my turn."

Like I said, I was always looking at Dinah's horrible shoes when she jumped. On the Monday after Thanksgiving vacation, she was at it again—ninety-one, ninety-two, ninety-three—and I was watching. It was the first day of the week, so my shoes still had their Sunday shine. Compared to Dinah's they looked brand new. As I watched, a feeling started to grow in me. I didn't know what it was at first, but it kept growing and growing until I thought I would burst.

Then the words that fit the feeling came to me: I wanted to give Dinah my shoes.

I would make the offer. Then I would take off my shoes, being careful to untie the laces first. Dinah wouldn't bother with her laces. She never did. She would just slip her feet from her shoes, then hold the shoes out to me. For a minute, we'd stand there looking at each other, then we'd exchange.

Her shoes would be way too big for me, but even so, the scrunched up backs would gouge into my heels uncomfortably. It wouldn't matter though. I would have done something that was important to me. Something my heart said I should do, not just something that was expected.

Momma certainly wouldn't expect me to come home in Dinah's shoes. She would be startled at first, then she would be furious. Her wide, smiley mouth would priss up. Her eyes would widen. Then she would grab me by the arm. "What did you say you did?" she would demand.

"I traded shoes with Dinah," I would repeat in a soft, uncertain voice.

"You traded your *new* shoes?"

"Yes'm."

"For *these?*"

"Yes'm?"

"Why?"

"Because . . . because she needs them more than I do."

Nice-looking shoes meant a lot to Momma. If our shoes looked nice, then we were doing okay. My feet in Dinah's shoes would mean something awful. It would be like saying Momma neglected me. So that's why if I gave Dinah my shoes, Momma would have to go over to her house and get them back. And then she wouldn't talk to me for a week.

It seemed like a big price to pay for doing something I wanted to do. Still, the feeling in my heart was stretching my ribs wider and wider. I had to do it! I needed to do it!

And I couldn't.

I couldn't give Dinah my shoes any more than Momma could teach the gospel to Dinah's family.

Momma was excited about teaching them when she first got the idea. But when it came down to actually going over to the Rock Pile and knocking on the door, she couldn't bring herself to do it. Although Daddy kept trying to set a time for it, she always found some way to change the subject. I guess it was easier for Momma to *talk* about missionary work. She was real good at that. Whenever we got a letter from Alma, we could count on also getting a missionary sermon from Momma, usually during dinner. Why, just a few days earlier, she had delivered one.

"Ask for a special blessing on Alma," Momma had told Lorenzo as he was getting ready to bless the food at supper.

After the blessing, Daddy asked, "What's going on with Alma?"

"Nothing." Momma said, starting the twice-baked potatoes. Then she added, "That's why he's down. He's been tracting for months now, and the only thing he's got to show for it is sore feet and worn-out shoes."

"That's a bit of an exaggeration, Faye. He has been able to teach some people."

"I know, but right now he feels like he's a failure because he doesn't have any converts. That's why we all need to write him a letter."

"What do you want us to say?" asked Lorenzo.

"Oh, something like 'Success isn't measured in the number of converts you make. If you're doing your best, you're successful.'"

"Right. I'll put that in my letter," Lorenzo said, grinning at Cheryl.

"Real cute. What's left for me to say, if you put all that in your letter?" Cheryl asked.

"Write what you feel," said Momma.

"I feel glad that it's not me getting the door slammed in my face. But I don't suppose that's what you had in mind."

Momma put down her fork. "For heaven's sake, no! Say something like 'No matter how difficult it gets, you'll be blessed for doing the Lord's work.' Isn't that right, Orrin?"

Daddy had nodded. He had looked straight at Momma and after a bit she had dropped her eyes.

I thought about that incident all the way home on the bus, and no matter how I tried to work it out, it didn't make sense. If Momma believed what she said about doing the Lord's work—no matter whether it turned out right or not—then she should have been on her way to visit Mr. and Mrs. Knotts long ago.

When I got off the bus, I went straight into the living room where Momma was working on a quilt for Alma. Without even saying "hi" first, I asked, "When are you and Daddy going to talk to Dinah's family about the gospel?"

Momma's head snapped up. "What?"

"You said they needed the gospel, didn't you?"

"Yes."

"Didn't you mean it?"

"Of course I did," said Momma, jabbing the needle through the quilt.

"Then?"

"I'll talk to your Daddy about it tonight."

"Thank you, Momma," I said in a softer voice.

She didn't say, "You're welcome."

But Momma kept her word. She and Daddy had a long talk after I went to bed. I know because I sneaked down where I could hear them. Before Cheryl caught me and sent me back upstairs, I heard part of their conversation.

"But Orrin, we can't just appear on their doorstep and announce that we've come to teach them. Really! You hardly ever talk to Asa about anything except business, and I haven't spoken to Idabelle in three years."

Momma mumbled something, then her voice rose again. "I don't think I can do it, if you want to know the truth. I'd probably throw up the minute I stepped foot into the place."

"Not a very brave missionary, are you?" Daddy chuckled.

That was far as they got before Cheryl made me go up to bed. The next morning, I didn't so much as get my mouth open when Momma gave me such a hard look that I didn't dare ask her what she and Daddy had decided to do.

Sometime during the spring of third grade, I think it was just before Easter, Momma got her courage up. She and Daddy went over to the Knotts place after dinner and came back a little while later. Momma was talking as they came in the back door.

"I told you it wouldn't work."

"Sure it will. We've just got to give it time."

"Time won't change a thing. Asa and Idabelle were as uncomfortable as we were. They don't really want us to

74

come back again, they only agreed because Dinah seemed to want us to. I declare, I don't understand what the tie is between Letty and Dinah."

"Whatever it is, it's good."

Momma snorted. Then she spied me. "Did you get your ears full?"

"Y-yes," I answered truthfully.

"I hope you liked what you heard."

"Momma, if you don't want to go back to their place, you could have them come here—"

Momma laughed, but it wasn't a happy sound. "Child, you are a trial to my faith. You and Dinah Knotts."

"We're not trying to be."

"I know," said Momma. Her voice was soft again, and her mouth was wide and almost turned up at the corners. "I know."

CHAPTER ELEVEN

Momma was saved by the coming of spring and the beginning of the planting season. Living on a farm like we did and having a big cattle operation meant that from April to November, everybody was pretty busy. And not just us Millers. Dinah's family was out working long hours, too. Picking rock, I guessed. It was just easier all the way around to let the missionary lessons go for a while.

That didn't mean Momma was spared contact with them, though. It seemed like everywhere we turned, one of the Knotts family was there.

Bob had quit trying to graduate. Even before school was out, he got a full-time job in town at the Husky Oil filling station. That was where we always went. Bob did a good job and was always pleasant, but I could tell Momma was uncomfortable when he serviced the car.

Henry seemed to be making a career out of bringing in "varmits" that he could get a bounty on. And since Daddy was still treasurer of the "Varmit" Control Board, Henry brought them over to us. It would take some time for Daddy to do the paperwork and make out the check, so Henry usually talked to Lorenzo while he waited on the porch. When Lorenzo found out that Henry shared his interest in learning how to reload shells, he talked Daddy into buying the equipment and teaching them how to do it.

Momma certainly didn't look happy whenever Henry was in our garage with Daddy and Lorenzo, melting the lead and tamping the powder in the reloading process. One night, she even accused Daddy of spending so much time with Henry that he was getting a drawl.

"It's true," she said. "You're starting to sound just like Asa Knotts."

Daddy grinned, which made Momma even madder.

Me spending time with Dinah at Uncle Orvel's didn't improve her disposition any.

That started the day Daddy dropped me off at the Shoe and Saddle Shop so I could talk to Uncle Orvel while Daddy did his business.

But Uncle Orvel was already talking to someone—Dinah Knotts.

I don't know why, but it made me furious to see him giving her the attention I thought was reserved only for me. I stood by the door, seething, until Buck shouted, "How do, Letty!"

"Okay," I mumbled.

Uncle Orvel gave his customary greeting, then he said, "Come on over. Our friend Dinah has been keeping me company."

Dinah smiled shyly. She looked at me out of the corners of her eyes as if she wasn't sure how I was going to react.

I wasn't sure how I was going to react. First of all, I had never really thought of Dinah as my friend. Second, I didn't like finding out that Uncle Orvel considered her to be his friend. But then Uncle Orvel gave me one of his wonderful smiles and a hug that was just as warm and comforting as his hugs had always been. It seemed Uncle Orvel could like both me and Dinah. It was a great relief.

Uncle Orvel was putting a new sole on a pair of boots for Mr. Knotts. He let us watch while he finished, then he said, "Well, are you just going to stand there?"

Dinah and I looked at each other. We had no idea what he was talking about.

"If you're going to hang around, you might as well do something. Here, come on back."

Dinah and I walked around the counter, then Uncle Orvel put us up on some stools where there was work space. He put some scrap leather, some stamping tools, and a punch in front of us. And before Mr. Knotts came back, Dinah and I had each made a little coin purse.

Uncle Orvel was a real artist in leather. Repairing shoes was only part of his business. He made most of his money doing custom work for people who saw the ads he put in magazines like *Gun World*, *Field and Stream*, and *Farm Journal*. He made everything from boots to hats, to purses. That's why he had all the scrap leather around.

He was real patient with Dinah and me. He didn't care how long it took us to do something. If we had a problem, he just helped us solve it. And if there was a part we couldn't do ourselves, he took over. Like when it came time to punch the holes for the lacing, we weren't strong enough and he had to do it for us.

Those coin purses looked great. "Look what we did!" Dinah cried when her daddy walked into the shop.

"That's right purty, gal," said Mr. Knotts, turning it over in his hand. "And how much will I owe you for it, Orvel?"

Uncle Orvel shook his head. "Not a thing, Asa. It's only scrap leather."

Mr. Knotts eyed Uncle Orvel. "You sure?"

"Yes, indeed."

About that time, Daddy walked in the door. "Howdy, Buck. Howdy, Asa. And no, I wouldn't like to be laughed at," said Daddy before Uncle Orvel could open his mouth.

Daddy examined the coin purses we had made. "That's good work, Letty. And you, too, Dinah. I guess maybe you ought to make a couple more. We'd each like one, wouldn't we, Asa?"

Mr. Knotts nodded. And before I could blink, Daddy was leaning against the counter, talking to Asa Knotts like they were old friends. Like they were neighbors. Uncle Orvel was putting in his two bits' worth, and pretty soon Buck Wellington pulled up a chair. Dinah and I had nothing to do but watch and listen as Daddy sucked his toothpick, Buck chewed and spat, and the four of them carried on for about an hour.

Finally, Daddy said, "Hey, Letty. Reckon we'd better get going before your momma takes it in mind to skin the both of us."

Mr. Knotts laughed.

"Orrin, Asa, you bring these girls in on Thursdays," said Uncle Orvel. "We'll whip up a couple more of those coin purses. And I bet we can figure out some other things to do, as well. How does that sound?"

Dinah smiled. "Great!" I squeaked.

"One of us ought to be able to do that. We could trade off, couldn't we?" asked Daddy.

Mr. Knotts nodded. And I thought of how Momma would react to the idea of me riding into town in a rattly pickup.

Daddy must have had a talk with Momma. I mean a real talk. Most of the time, Daddy didn't lock horns with Momma, but when things were real important, he would take a stand and not back down. He must have taken a stand on this, because one of the things I did the summer between the third and fourth grade was go to the Shoe and Saddle Shop with Dinah. And every other week or so, I rode with Dinah and her daddy in their pickup.

We had a great time. In fact, that summer I saw more of Dinah than I had during any other summer, even though she had never yet set foot on our place. Not only did we visit Uncle Orvel, but we went swimming together. And a couple of times, Dinah and I rode up to the range with Daddy and Mr. Knotts, who was running some of his cows with ours. Once we even got to stay overnight.

Except for the fact that Momma stopped smiling, it would have been a perfect summer. It was probably a good thing we didn't know that when school started in the fall, we were going to get Mrs. Reigert for fourth grade.

CHAPTER TWELVE

Mrs. Reigert was standing in front of the classroom when Dinah and I walked in. Right off, my eyes flew to her crinkled reddish hair and her eyebrows, which were pulled into a scowl. The scowl matched the turned-down corners of her mouth.

Then I remembered Lorenzo's words: "Mrs. Reigert's real mean."

He was right about that. Mrs. Reigert *was* mean.

I found that out when she asked the class to read for her. "Anderson, Polly! You read the first paragraph," she snapped.

Polly read well, I thought. But Mrs. Reigert didn't even say "That's nice," or "Thank you," or even "I'm sure you can do better." She just scowled.

Right then, I wished we had Mrs. Morehead again. While her brand of politeness and encouragement might not have lead to great progress, at least it made us feel good.

"Banks, Janet!"

"Bucher, William!"

"Erickson, Michael!"

One by one, we stood up to read. One by one, she shot us down. It was all too easy. I could have told her you don't need a canon to knock a Campbell's soup can off the fence post.

The whole last year, Mrs. Morehead and I had pretended that I was doing okay. She had been willing to gloss over my problem by letting me read out of easy books, first-grade books. I was getting pretty good at that level, but Mrs. Reigert was expecting me to read out of something way too hard for me. I knew I couldn't do it. There was no point in even trying.

Dinah finished her paragraph and passed the book back to me. Mrs. Reigert checked her seating chart. "Miller, Loretta! Start reading on page seventeen."

I stood up. "My name is Letty, and I can't."

"I don't believe in shortening names, Loretta. Now, what do you mean you can't?"

"I can't."

"You don't remember the page number?" Mrs. Reigert asked. "It's page seventeen."

"I remember what page. That's not the problem."

"What exactly is the problem, Loretta?"

"I don't know how."

"Come now, pick up the book."

Mrs. Reigert moved to the head of the aisle where I stood. I picked up the book and opened it to page seventeen.

"Read the first paragraph."

I looked at the page. There was nothing but words from top to bottom. I say words, only because I knew they were words. What I saw were only lines. Some separate, some jumbled. All impossible.

"Loretta, begin!"

I just stood there.

Mrs. Reigert slammed her book down on the front desk. My eyes flew from the page to her face. It was red and angry. "What is your problem?" she demanded.

"She can't read," whispered Dinah. "At least not out of this book."

Mrs. Reigert pointed a finger directly at Dinah. "I did not speak to you, young lady. Loretta Miller, sit down." And on she went to "Nesbitt, Gloria!"

In the next few days, she tested us on math and spelling and social studies and other stuff. When she finished, she announced, "This class is a disaster. I have never had such a poor fourth-grade class in my whole life. In fact, I have even had third-grade classes that did better than you. I am appalled! Especially with your level of reading." She shook her crimped head. "I don't know what to do with you."

That was a lie, because she knew exactly what she was going to do with us. She was going to make our lives miserable.

The first thing she did was separate a bunch of us from the rest of the class. She instructed us to empty our desks and come to the front of the class. Then she made us sit down across the front row, and said, "You're here because by rights you have no business in fourth grade at all."

Besides me, the other front-row dumbbells were Clyde Robertson, Mike Erickson, and Dinah.

"How come Wattsie Pottsie isn't up here with us?" I whispered to Dinah. "You're better than she is at both math and reading."

"Are you kidding? She could be a re-tard and Mrs. Reigert wouldn't put her up here. Look at her."

I looked. She was sitting all sweet and smiley, her legs crossed right at the lace trim of her anklets. Her black patent leather Sunday shoes were like mirrors. Her dress was tucked and ruffled, and her red hair was done up in perfect ringlets. Dinah was right.

I didn't think Mrs. Reigert had to make such a big deal out of putting us on the front row. Still, I would have forgiven her for saying out loud that we were the slowest in the class, if she had really wanted to help us get better. Or if she had put Wattsie Pottsie up with us where she belonged.

But when it came right down to it, Mrs. Reigert didn't like us. She only wanted us up front where she could see everything we did wrong.

"Clyde! Stop picking your scab."

"Dinah, go wash your hands, they're filthy. No, before you go, hold them up so everybody can see the way you come to school."

"Loretta! I can't believe you still don't know how to spell *tomorrow*. Come up here and write it twenty-five times on the blackboard. Then we'll test you again."

I could have told her it wouldn't make any difference. I could copy anything that was in front of me. The letters might not be even or pretty, but they would be right. The thing is, there was no guarantee I would be able to write the word five minutes later. I did what Mrs. Reigert told me to, though. I didn't have any choice.

After recess that same day, she called me up to the blackboard and said, "Write the word *tomorrow*."

Frantically, I looked to the side of the board where I had already written it twenty-five times. She had erased it during recess.

"Write the word *tomorrow*, and be snappy about it!" she repeated.

I closed my eyes and tried to see what that word looked like. I couldn't picture it at all. So I tried to sound it out. The result was: *t-u-m-a-r-o*.

"*T−O*," whispered Dinah urgently.

I quickly corrected the vowel.

"Another *O*!"

I changed the *A* for an *O*.

"Two *R*'s! And a *W*," said Dinah as loudly as she dared. I heard her and added the *R*'s and the *W*.

"See, Loretta, I told you that you could do it," said Mrs. Reigert.

Dinah saved me a lot that year. That's why I felt so bad about what happened. I don't think it was all my fault. Really, I think it was Mrs. Reigert's fault. If she hadn't been so mean . . . But she was, and the person she picked on most was me.

"All right, class, put your things away. It's time for art. No, not you, Letty. You have to work on your reading. We have to get you beyond the second-grade reader somehow!"

"Can't I draw, too? I did real good on my math."

"That may be so, but your reading is still very poor." She put her hands on her hips and looked down at me. "All it takes is work. Anybody who can do their math as well as you can should be the best reader in the class. You're just being lazy. Or stubborn. I'm not sure which. But I declare, it's a real disgrace to your parents that you are in the front row."

I bent my head over my desk so she wouldn't see I was crying.

"Class," Mrs. Reigert instructed, "take out your crayons. The first thing I want you to do is fill your page with bands of the brightest colors you can find."

I opened the book Mrs. Reigert had handed me.

"Now, cover the whole page with black. It should look like this when you're finished," Mrs. Reigert said, holding up an example. "There shouldn't be any color at all showing."

I turned the page. There were no pictures to look at, so I made a pretense of reading while I tried to get a glimpse of Dinah's artwork.

"We're at the fun part," Mrs. Reigert was saying. "By scratching off the black in a design, you can make a picture. Like this. It can be anything you want it to be. Mountains, trees, animals—pick whatever you like."

I glanced at page eight and then looked at the picture on page nine.

Dinah nudged me softly with her elbow. "See?" she whispered as she slid her finished picture onto the top of my desk. It was a horse with a flying mane and tail. It looked like Silver when the Lone Ranger rides him fast.

"Keep it," said Dinah shyly.

That night, I sat with her on the bus.

"You should tell your ma," she said, wiping her nose with the back of her hand.

"You should use a Kleenex," I said, handing her one from my school bag.

"I know, but I never have one. You should still tell your ma."

"I guess so. Thanks for the picture."

She smiled. "It's not very good. You're the best draw-er in class."

"I am?"

"And the best at math. It's not fair for Mrs. Reigert to put you on the front row just because you can't read."

"Teachers don't have to be fair. They can do anything they want." I thought for a minute, then I added, "You shouldn't be in the front row, either."

Dinah shook her head from side to side, but her eyes were gleaming.

"I'll tell you a secret," I continued. "I know I can't read. That's a fact, and maybe for that, I deserve to be on the front row. But you read real good. You're better at reading and math than old Wattsie Pottsie, and she's not sitting right under Mrs. Reigert's nose. If you ask me, the only reason you're there is because your last name is Knotts. I may be word-blind, but Mrs. Reigert is people-blind."

CHAPTER THIRTEEN

If Mrs. Reigert didn't want to see, Momma didn't want to hear. I found that out when I repeated my description to her that evening. "I may be word-blind, but Mrs. Reigert is people-blind."

"Letty, children shouldn't talk about adults in that manner," began Momma, then she turned to me with questioning eyes. "What do you mean, she's blind?"

"Mrs. Reigert can't see that Dinah isn't dumb, and that I can't learn how to read."

Momma sighed. "That again. We've been over it a thousand times, and I'm getting pretty tired of it, Lor-etta Miller. If you can learn to do math, you can learn to read, and reading is more important. You have to learn to read."

It was a funny thing about Momma. Part of the time, she totally ignored the fact that I was still having problems with my reading. She didn't like having a daughter who couldn't read, any more than she liked having a brother who couldn't. She didn't like having to explain when people asked, "How is Letty doing in school?" Then, when she did admit that there was a problem, she went overboard, thinking that just willpower and hard work could solve it.

That was almost true. I had gotten a little better over the years, as a result of Uncle Orvel's help and Momma's determination. But willpower couldn't change the fact that being anxious or worried about reading made my problem even worse. And on the front row of Mrs. Reigert's class, I was always anxious.

I had sense enough not to try to explain it to Momma, though. Every day, I had more and more thoughts I couldn't say. Thoughts I had to hide away inside myself.

It was sort of like when Daddy fills up the silage pit to make feed for our livestock. The chopped corn is nice and sweet and green when he puts it in, but it gets all stinky and hot after it's been in there a while. I had my own pit. The thoughts were fresh when I put them in, but they were getting nasty, just like silage does. And they were filling me with hot, stinky feelings.

In the middle of all that, we kept getting long, excited letters from Alma. He had learned enough French to give discussions and buy groceries and read the subway schedule. He kept saying how wonderful his mission was and how much he felt the Spirit. I had been waiting for the Spirit ever since he baptized me—but with no luck. I didn't like hearing about the family he had converted and how happy they were. It didn't seem fair for them to be happy and not me.

"Why don't you write Alma a letter?" Momma asked one day. "I'm sending him a box of homemade fudge. I could put it right in the box. It'll be a surprise for him."

You bet it will! I thought. The kind of letter I had in mind wasn't at all what Momma was imagining.

I sat right down and started writing.

"Do you need any help?" asked Momma, coming to peer over my shoulder.

"No. I'm doing all right," I lied.

I was just about finished when Daddy sat down beside me and put his arm around me.

"How's it coming, kiddo?" he asked.

"See for yourself," I said. Showing the letter to Daddy wasn't the same as showing it to Momma. I knew Daddy would understand.

"Are you sure this is what you want to send to Alma?"

"Yes, but I'd like you to correct my spelling."

"If you're sure."

"I'm sure."

When we got done, I put the letter in an envelope and sealed it.

"I'm so proud of you," said Momma when she saw the envelope lying in the box.

I didn't think she would be proud if she had read it herself. What I had written was this:

Dear Alma,

I'm glad you are having a good time. I'm not. I've been waiting for the Holy Ghost's cook fire, but I haven't felt it yet. The closest I come is when I'm mad. But then I'm hot, and that's not the same thing.

You keep saying how people's lives get changed by the Gospel. Well, I thought you'd like to know that Dinah's still on the Rock Pile.

I think you're all wet.

Your sister,

Loretta Miller

Alma wrote back. He said I should have patience, and that I should remember that he loved me. And that God loved me.

It sounded nice, but I needed more than that.

A miracle was what I needed.

So things went from bad to worse real fast. I felt like those movie stars who were going to get squashed in the horror show I had seen at the Rainbow Theater. When I felt like that, I got all hot and red inside. Then I would do something mean, like hit Joe or drop a plate on purpose or swear in Sunday School class. I knew it didn't help matters, but I had to do something or I would blow apart.

And that was exactly what happened the day I x-ed out the pages in *Little House on the Prairie*.

That day, Mrs. Reigert told me to look up the word *conversation*. I got the dictionary and opened it to a random page.

"Well, have you found it?" she asked.

"No."

"Hurry up."

Con-ver-sa-tion, I said to myself, trying to figure out how it might be spelled. Logically, it should have started with a *K*. So I turned to the *K*'s. But what came next? To me, that *ah* sound could only be made by an *A*. But then again, I knew spelling was tricky. It could just as easily be made by an *O* or a *U*. So I was stumped.

"Have you got it?"

"Not yet."

"*Conversation!*" Mrs. Reigert said real loud, as if by shouting it she could make me understand.

And so it went all morning. While the other fourth-graders went from reading to math to drawing an Indian Paintbrush, which was the state flower, I sat with the dictionary on my lap. Periodically, Mrs. Reigert would charge down on me, demanding to know why I hadn't looked up *conversation* yet. My salvation finally came with the lunch bell.

It was a good thing, too, because all morning long, I could feel myself getting redder and redder and hotter and hotter. I was so red hot, I couldn't eat. I barely even looked at the lunch on the tray before I tossed it into the trash and went out on the playground.

I must have looked grim as I walked around with my teeth clenched and my fists cocked, because most of the kids moved out of my way. The ones who didn't, got smacked or poked. I just couldn't keep my hands from flashing out at anybody who stayed within striking distance. I had made the rounds twice when the playground monitor grabbed my hand from behind just as I was getting ready to let another one fly.

"That's enough of that!" She said, dragging me to the building. "You sit right here," she ordered, pointing to a stool that was placed inside the door, "and I'll take you to the principal's office later."

For a while, she kept looking in my direction to make sure I hadn't moved. Then some little kid fell off the merry-go-round and started screaming bloody murder. That got her attention, all right. While she was taking him in the direction of the nurse's office, I slipped off the stool and started wandering the quiet halls. When I saw that the door to my classroom was open and that Mrs. Reigert was nowhere to be seen, I got the idea.

Just thinking about it made my ears burn and my insides shake, but I walked straight into the room and over to the corner reserved for everybody but me. Even Dinah and Clyde had earned the chance to do something fun in that corner, but I knew I never would. No matter how hard I worked, Mrs. Reigert would always find something else for me to do.

She couldn't stop me from going to the corner now. I crept over to it and picked up the first book I saw. It was *Little House on the Prairie*, the book that Mrs. Reigert read out loud during our morning milk break. We had already finished *Little House in the Big Woods* that way. I loved those books. I could hardly wait for each new installment. That didn't stop me, though. More than anything, I wanted to get back at Mrs. Reigert.

I got my black Crayola crayon out and opened up *Little House on the Prairie*. Covering the first page and part of the second was a picture of the Ingallses' wagon moving over the prairie. Their dog Jack was following along behind. I turned the page. There was nothing but words on the next two pages. I drew a big, black X through each page, pressing down on my crayon so hard that I cracked it. The only thing that kept it together was the paper label.

Methodically, I drew big black X's through as many pages as I dared. I skipped all the pages that had pictures, though. It never occurred to me to x them out, because pictures were my clues to the world. Every time I turned a page, my heart pounded faster and harder, and when the warning bell rang, I nearly jumped out of my skin.

Quickly, I put the book back on the shelf and the crayon back in my desk. Then I sneaked back out of the room and onto the stool. I barely made it. I had just folded my arms when the playground monitor came in to check on me.

"Oh, you're still here. Well, go on to class," she said. "You've been good, so we'll let it pass this time. But if I ever catch you hitting kids again, I won't be so easy on you."

I spent the rest of the day dreading yet anticipating the moment when Mrs. Reigert would find the ruined book. I imagined how I would stand up to her, boldly saying, "I did it. Any teacher as rotten as you deserves to have her book ruined." But the only thing I got in trouble for that day was hitting people: it wasn't until the next day during milk break that Mrs. Reigert discovered my deed.

I knew she would. My hands shook as I got my little bottle of milk and walked back to my seat. Mrs. Reigert waited until everybody was ready, then she opened the book. The smile that was on her face froze and dropped right along with her jaw as she saw what I'd done. For a minute, there was dead silence in the class. Then she turned the book around so that everyone could see what she had just seen. There were shocked gasps as the class reacted.

Mrs. Reigert stood up, her eyes huge with fury. "Who did this?" she asked in an awful voice.

Nobody peeped.

"I want to know, right now!" she yelled.

Sweat was popping out on her forehead and her face was red.

"Now!" screamed Mrs. Reigert.

My eyes flashed to her eyes, and I cowered just looking at her. I had never seen an adult get so angry. It terrified me. When I covered the words with heavy, black lines, I had imagined that I would admit it was my handiwork and thumb my nose with a who-cares gesture. Mrs. Reigert's bug-eyed stare drove that thought right out of my head. To admit my guilt would be to put myself in mortal danger.

Suddenly, Mrs. Reigert focused on Dinah. "You did it, didn't you!" she cried, advancing on Dinah.

No, no! I did it, my brain shrieked, but my lips were caught between my teeth and no sound came out.

"I might have known. Why they let you Knotts children come to school is beyond me. It doesn't do any good, does it?"

"Tell her you didn't do it," I whispered frantically. Dinah looked at me sideways and in a flash of understanding, I knew . . . that she knew . . . that I was the one. But she didn't say anything, not one word.

"You did it, admit it!" Mrs. Reigert demanded.

Dinah just looked at her hands.

"Stand up, you horrible child!"

Dinah stood.

Mrs. Reigert raised the book, and for a moment, I thought she was going to crash it down on Dinah's head. Then, ever so slowly, with shaking hands, she lowered it.

"Go to the principal's office. Stay there. I don't want you back in this room today, and maybe never."

Dinah's face looked like a soap carving, all flat and white, but she didn't cry and she didn't tell on me. She just walked out of the room with courage so great I thought my heart would break.

When the last bell of the day rang, I dashed from the room and out to the bus. Dinah was already sitting in it, red-eyed and silent. As usual, she didn't have a tissue and when she rubbed the back of her hand across her nose, she smeared stuff on her cheek.

I sat down beside her and handed her a Kleenex. After a while I asked, "How did you know?"

"Easy," she said with a shudder. "You didn't mess up the pictures, only the words. Nobody else in class really hates words but you."

"If you figured it out, how come she didn't?"

"You said it. She's people-blind."

"Why didn't you tell on me?"

"Because you're my only friend."

CHAPTER FOURTEEN

As the bus went over the rise just before my place, Dinah said, "I have to pay for the book. It cost seventy-five cents."

I don't know why I hadn't thought of that before, but of course, someone would have to pay for the book. And Dinah certainly couldn't.

She studied her dirty nails. "How many magpie feet is seventy-five cents?"

"Twelve," I said without hesitation. I *was* good at math.

"Henry got that many in a weekend, once. Maybe he'll help me—"

"But that means you'll have to tell him what happened!"

"He'll know anyway. Miss Delmar is going to drive out tonight to talk to Ma and Pa."

"Oh no! When?"

" 'Bout eight o'clock. Then I reckon my Pa'll whup me."

We stared at each other. Neither one of us had thought much about the consequences of what we had done that day, we had just followed our feelings. Only, the feelings I had followed were the worst kind, and hers were the best. She had tried to save me from Mrs. Reigert's wrath, and I had let her. We hadn't thought about what it would cost Dinah. Things were getting out of hand, and I didn't see any way to stop what was going to happen.

Unless I told on myself.

Before I had a chance to pursue that thought any fur-
ther, the bus came to a stop. "Dinah—" I began.

"Are you going to get off or what?" Joe said, standing
beside me. "Come on. Everybody's waiting on you."

I grabbed my school bag and rushed out of the bus.

"What's the matter with you, anyway?" Joe demanded
when he caught up with me.

"Nothing."

"My foot. There is too something wrong, and you better fess up or I'll tell Momma and Daddy."

"Oh, yeah? Just what are you going to tell them, huh?"

"I don't know . . . that you're acting funny."

"That won't get you very far. They think I act funny all
the time. Now you leave me alone, you little brat!" I cried,
and ran out to the barn. In the comfort of the warm, musty
darkness, I tried to figure out what to do.

Miss Delmar was going to drive up the Knotts lane at
eight o'clock. Dinah would never tell on me, I was sure of
that. If I was going to tell on myself, I had to do it before
eight o'clock.

Then a horrible thought occurred to me. Dinah would
probably have to talk to her momma and daddy before
then. I had even less time than I thought. I knew Mrs.
Knotts wouldn't be home till later, but what about Mr.
Knotts? He could have been sitting at the kitchen table
right then, asking Dinah why Miss Delmar was going to
come.

Dinah's last words came back to me: "Then I reckon
my Pa'll whup me."

Mr. Knotts was so big that his belly pushed out the
front of his coveralls until they almost burst. And his hands
were like rubber gloves filled up with too much water. If he
ever got mad, why then . . .

A vision of Asa Knotts rose up before me. He was bear-
ing down on Dinah with his big hands outstretched. I started

to scream. I tore out of the barn screaming, "Momma! Momma, where are you?!"

Momma came running from the house when she heard me. "What's the matter?" she cried, grabbing me by the arm and looking me over.

"She's done something she oughtn't to have," said Joe, who'd been hanging around just waiting to make trouble for me.

He needn't have bothered. He couldn't come anywhere near getting me into the kind of trouble I was going to bring on myself.

"Is that true?" asked Momma.

I was still shaking from the vision I'd had, but I nodded.

She stepped back disapprovingly. "What an awful thing, to give me such a fright like that. I thought you were hurt!"

"I'm not hurt, but Dinah will be—Mr. Knotts is going to kill her!"

"For heaven's sake, child, save that for later when I have some time. I was just getting ready to make fruitcake for Christmas dinner. It has to sit six weeks, you know."

"But he is, he is!" I cried, pulling on her apron. "Dinah's going to tell him that she marked up *Little House on the Prairie* with black crayons, and that she has to pay seventy-five cents for it, and Miss Delmar's going to go out there at eight o'clock, and maybe she won't let Dinah go to school anymore, but Dinah didn't do it! It's all my fault!"

"What?"

"I did it! I'm the one who ruined the book," I gasped. "Dinah knew I was the only one who would have made a mess like that, because I'm the only one who hates words. So she said she did it, because she knows Mrs. Reigert hates me, and she wanted to save me. Only now, Mr. Knotts is going to kill Dinah because the book costs seventy-five cents, and they don't have any money, and it would take twelve pair of magpie feet, and—"

"Lor-etta Miller, you stop that right now!"

"You have to save Dinah," I screamed, pounding at Momma with my fists.

Momma shook me then, and when I didn't stop screaming, she slapped me, hard. I shuddered and swallowed my tears.

"Now." Momma said that one word, then took a deep breath. "You are going to come into the house. You are going to sit down. Then you are going to tell me what this is all about."

"Yes'm."

"And you, Joe! You get out to the barn and start your chores. And don't be in any hurry to get them done, you hear?"

It was hard to talk, because I was shaking so bad. Also, my nose was running. But I told her. I told her how Mrs. Reigert liked to make people feel bad, and how she always picked on us kids in the first row.

"And she hates me most of all. She thinks I'm a disgrace to my family because I can't read. She figures if she makes me feel bad enough, she can make me learn. But I can't," I ended on a wail.

"Letty, what happened today?"

"It didn't happen today, it happened yesterday, only nobody found out about it until today."

Momma nodded, but I could tell she wanted me to get on with it.

"She, she . . . " I searched my vocabulary and came up with a big word that I thought might be right. "She *humiliated* me! And Momma, it made me get all hot inside. I wanted to hurt her back." I started sobbing again, so the words came out sort of jerky. "I sneaked . . . into the classroom and I took a . . . black crayon and I drew big . . . black . . . lines through all the pages of . . . *Little House on*

98

the *Prairie*. And Mrs. Reigert accused Dinah of doing it. And . . . I didn't tell her it was me!"

"Oh, child," said Momma, but instead of getting mad like I thought she would, she pulled me onto her lap where I could lay my head on her shoulder.

"I did something awful, Momma, and now Dinah is going to get it, and I'd rather get it myself."

Momma started rocking me back and forth, patting my hair. "I didn't know it was that bad," she murmured. "You tried to tell me, but I didn't believe it. I didn't want to believe it." She moved me out where she could look right into my eyes. "Now let's get this straight. Miss Delmar is going to go to the Knotts place tonight?"

"Yes'm. But I think Dinah will probably have to tell her daddy before then, and I'm scared . . . "

"What do you think we should do?"

I took a deep breath. I didn't want to say what I was going to say, but I had to. "Call Miss Delmar and tell her I did it, so she'll come here instead of to the Knotts. Then I have to go tell Dinah. But I'm not very brave. I don't want to have to do it."

"I think you're very brave," said Momma. She straightened up my dress a little and wiped the smudges off my face. Then she wiped the tears off her own.

"I'm sorry, Momma. I didn't mean to be bad."

"I know that, Letty."

She gave me another hug, then she got all businesslike. She looked up Miss Delmar's number and gave it to the operator.

"Miss Delmar? This is Faye Miller. My daughter Letty has something she wants to tell you."

Momma held out the phone to me. When I hesitated, she smiled at me and gave a little nod. I took the phone in hand, and I confessed.

There was a long pause on the other end of the line, then Miss Delmar said, "Let me talk to your mother again."

I could tell from Momma's end of the conversation that Miss Delmar was still going to be driving out our road tonight, only she would be coming to my house instead of to Dinah's. Momma hung up, then she sighed. "I sure wish Dinah's folks had a phone," she said.

I couldn't believe it. She was saying exactly what I was thinking. I didn't want to talk to Mr. Knotts face-to-face, but I had no choice in the matter.

We were about to walk out the door, when suddenly my Momma started to cry. She just leaned against the door frame and let the tears roll down her cheeks. At first, I was bewildered, but then I figured out what her tears were about. "Momma," I said softly, "you don't have to go to the Knotts place with me if you don't want to."

Momma made a funny noise that sounded like a laugh and a sob together. Then she smiled a little. "And you were worried about not being brave. Wait until I wash my face, then we'll go together."

Once when Momma got after Alma for driving too fast, she said he was driving like "a bat out of hell." I couldn't figure out what she meant at the time, because the only bats I knew of were baseball bats. It sounded fine, though, and it became my favorite phrase.

Well, that afternoon, Momma was driving like a bat out of hell. She was trying to smile, but her jaw was stiff and her hands gripped the steering wheel so tightly that her knuckles were white. All that tension went on down her leg to her foot, which was pressing the gas pedal right down to the floor. She just couldn't help driving fast.

On the way over, I kept hoping that we wouldn't have to go inside the Knotts house. So I was real glad when Dinah opened the door to see who had come up the lane.

She looked at me and then at Momma and didn't say a word. She wasn't sure how much I had told Momma.

Finally, Momma broke the silence.

"Hello, Dinah," she said.

"Hi."

"Is your mother at home?"

"She's still at work."

"How about your father?"

"He's out feeding the cows."

"Why don't you tell him we're here."

When they came around the corner of the house, Mr. Knotts had Dinah's hand in his. He *was* big, but he didn't look mean. I ducked my head, embarrassed at my previous hysterics.

"Afternoon," he said pleasantly to Momma, extending his hand right gentlemanlike. "Haven't seen you for a good piece."

Momma blushed. "You know how busy it gets . . . "

Mr. Knotts nodded, but he didn't help out Momma one bit. From the protection of her arm, I watched the two of them with great interest. I had never in my life seen Momma at a loss for words. Finally she cleared her throat and said, "I came over to talk to you about something that happened in school, today, Asa."

"Yes?"

"Something my daughter did. She defaced, uh, *ruined* a book by drawing black lines through the words. When Mrs. Reigert discovered it, Letty didn't come forward." Momma paused, then added reluctantly, "Mrs. Reigert blamed it on Dinah."

"I had to go to the principal's office," said Dinah, looking up into her father's big, red face.

"Why did you take the blame, gal?" Mr. Knotts asked.

"Mrs. Reigert wouldn't have changed her mind, even if I had told her the truth, Pa. Besides, I didn't want Letty to get into more trouble."

Mr. Knotts held Dinah close to him as he asked Momma, "What are you going to do about this?"

"Letty doesn't want Dinah to take the blame, Asa. That's what we're here to tell you. We've already called Miss Delmar, and Letty told her the truth. We'll talk to Mrs. Reigert as well, and something will have to be said in class to clear Dinah."

Mr. Knotts had been scowling and protectively holding Dinah's hand. When he heard what Momma and I had already done, his mouth relaxed into a little smile. "That's a change. My kids have been accused of lots of things since we moved here, and I doubt if they've done half of them. They know I'd let 'em have it if they didn't behave themselves."

While Momma and Mr. Knotts had been talking, the Knotts boys had silently joined the group in front of the sagging house. "Isn't that true, boys?" Mr. Knotts asked, and they nodded.

Momma had a puzzled look on her face. Mr. Knotts noticed it and said, "I guess you've been hearing different."

Momma had to nod.

"What did you hear?"

"About Bob . . . "

Bob shifted his feet, and I felt Momma stiffen. With a start, I realized that she was scared. " 'Twern't my fault," he said.

"What happened?" Momma asked.

Bob got red in the face.

"Go ahead and tell her," Mr. Knotts said.

Bob looked at the toes of his dusty shoes as he spoke. "It was Carl Draeger started it. He brought a squirt gun to class, and he squirted me. He squirted me *under* the table while we were in the library."

I gasped as I realized what Carl Draeger had been intending.

"When I stood up, Mr. Igelsrud started laughing at me, making fun of me. He wouldn't listen to me. So I . . . "

He didn't have to finish his sentence. Both Momma and I knew Mr. Igelsrud had ended up with a black eye and some sore ribs, and Bob had been suspended. Looking at Bob, who still hadn't lifted his eyes from his shoes, I thought Mr. Igelsrud got what he deserved and that Bob probably could have hurt him a lot worse if he had wanted to.

"Did you tell this to the principal?" asked Momma.

"Naw. Wouldn't do any good," said Bob.

"Then I will, when I talk to her tonight—"

Mr. Knotts shook his head. "No need to do that. You just clear up this business about the book."

"I will. Asa, I'm truly sorry."

"So am I," I blurted out when Momma nudged me with her elbow.

"I'm just glad my Dinah has such a good friend," said Mr. Knotts. "She's the only one of my kids who does."

Dinah had said that on the bus, and now Mr. Knotts was saying the same thing. I thought about it all the way home. For three-and-a-half years, I had sat by Dinah during school and gone swimming in the canal with her in the summer. But was I really her friend? Could she be my friend, even if I wasn't hers? Or did it have to go both ways?

There wasn't time to spend thinking about that riddle, though. There was barely enough time for supper and evening chores before Miss Delmar arrived.

CHAPTER FIFTEEN

The year that I was in fourth grade, I learned something important: bad things can sometimes lead to good things.

All I had wanted to do during that red-hot moment when I covered up the words in *Little House on the Prairie* was to get back at Mrs. Reigert. When I told on myself, I was only trying to save Dinah. I had had no idea what those events would lead to.

On our way back from Dinah's that day, Momma drove by the field where Daddy was turning the water and told him to come home as soon as he could. When he arrived, she sat us down in his office and made me tell what had happened all over again.

Daddy was upset, naturally, but he seemed more interested in what Momma had done than what I had done. "*You* drove over to the Knotts place?" he asked Momma. "You actually went over to the Rock Pile?"

"I didn't have much of a choice, did I?"

"Well, I'll be. I reckon that was a pretty hard thing to do."

Momma's mouth turned up a little. "You know what they say about pride going before a fall."

"How did Asa take it?"

"He was more understanding than I would have been. If I were Asa, I'd demand that Mrs. Reigert apologize to the whole family for what she said about them. But he won't."

"Why not?"

"He doesn't think it would do any good. Sometimes when people get an idea in their heads, it's almost impossible to change it. Orrin, you know all the things I heard about Bob and Mr. Igelsrud . . . I'm not sure it happened the way people say it did." Then Momma told Daddy what Bob had told her.

"Isn't that what I've been saying?" Daddy said. "Just shows you what things have built up to. Bob shouldn't have hit Mr. Igelsrud, that's for sure. But Mr. Igelsrud had no business letting Carl Draeger get away with what he did. As if that wasn't bad enough, Igelsrud added to it. But I'm not surprised."

Momma raised her eyebrows in a question.

"We've all had the attitude that Asa Knotts and his whole family were fair game because they talk different, they're poor, and they don't go to our church. But they are good people, Faye. That Dinah is a real thoroughbred."

"Yes," Momma admitted reluctantly. Then before Daddy could open his mouth, she added, "Just don't ask me to be bosom buddies with them. I'm not ready for that yet."

Daddy grinned and patted Momma's hand. "What do we do now?"

"I'm going to have a serious talk with Miss Delmar. If I have anything to do with it, Mrs. Reigert is going to stop bullying Dinah and Letty. And the other kids, too."

Momma paused and then turned to me. "But Letty, that doesn't mean you can just give up on reading."

"Why not?" I asked. "I can live without knowing how to read. It's being made fun of that I can't stand."

Momma shook her head and sighed. "All right," she said. "We'll start with that."

It took about half an hour to tell Miss Delmar every-thing that had been going on that year. She didn't look very happy about it. All the time I was talking, she sat there with her lips pulled down. The little mustache that had always fascinated me was pulled down, too. At first, I had to work at not looking at that mustache, but when I got going, I forgot it was even there.

Once in a while, she stopped me to ask a question, but mostly what she did was listen. When I ran out of things to say, Miss Delmar said, "Thank you, Letty. I'm glad you had the courage to come forward." Then Momma sent me off to bed.

I had no intention of going to bed, actually. I figured I'd get into my flannel nightgown and climb under the covers just long enough to convince everyone I had gone to sleep. Then, I planned to sneak out of bed and down the stairs to the dining room. The buffet on the dining room wall extended to the living room door. I was going to crawl under the buffet right up to the door where I could hear without being seen.

The plan would have worked, if I had stayed awake long enough to follow through with it. But I was exhausted by what I had been through that day, and the minute I got into bed, I fell asleep. I didn't stir until I awoke in the morn-ing to the smell of frying bacon.

"What happened, what happened?" I demanded as I ran into the kitchen.

"It's going to be taken care of," Momma said.

"What does that mean?"

"It means that Miss Delmar promised to talk to Mrs. Reigert last night after she got home. Mrs. Reigert will have to change her ways, I think."

"Can Miss Delmar really do that? I mean, make her change?"

"I think so. A little, at least."

Momma was right. That very morning, Mrs. Reigert had a new seating chart worked out. It was straight alphabetical. She read off our names one by one and pointed to the chair where she wanted us to sit. When she came to Dinah and me, she smiled so hard, her gums were showing. I don't think she would have been smiling at all, except for the fact that Miss Delmar stood at the door.

After we were all seated, Mrs. Reigert said, "Before we start our day's work, I have an apology to make. Yesterday, when no one would admit to ruining *Little House on the Prairie*, I mistakenly concluded that Dinah Knotts had done it. I sent her to Miss Delmar's office for discipline. That was my mistake. It wasn't Dinah." Mrs. Reigert drew a deep breath, then said, "I'm sorry, Dinah."

Her eyes skipped from Dinah to me. I could feel them boring into me, and I knew for sure that Mrs. Reigert hated me even more than ever. With a gleam of triumph, she said, "Loretta Miller has something she wants to say. Stand up, Loretta."

I stood and walked to the front of the class, but I didn't look out at my classmates. My eyes were glued to my saddle shoes. "I did it, and I'm sorry," I said. Then I sat down. All around me I heard whispers of "Why'd you *do* that?" and "How mean!" I put my hands over my ears so I wouldn't have to listen.

"Both of us made a mistake," said Mrs. Reigert. "Now everybody take out your math books and turn to page forty-five. Letty, if you have trouble reading the story problems I will be glad to help you."

My eyes flashed to Miss Delmar, who was still standing at the door. She nodded slightly and smiled. Then she left.

I did have trouble doing the problems, but it didn't have anything to do with reading. The tears in my eyes were making the page blurry. I hated having everybody in the class know that I had scribbled in *Little House on the Prairie*. All I wanted to do was get away from them all.

The minute the recess bell rang, I dashed out of the room and went straight to my favorite corner, the "inny" corner. I was squatting there with my chin on my knees when Dinah found me.

"How come you aren't playing?" she asked.

"'Cause. I don't want anybody to look at me. They all think I'm stupid."

Dinah grinned slyly. "What's so different about that?"

She so took me by surprise that all I could do was laugh. We were laughing together when Wattsie Pottsie came over to us.

"Want to jump rope, Dinah?" she asked.

"Sure," said Dinah. She started off with Wattsie Pottsie, then turned and said, "Come on, Letty."

I had barely gotten to my feet when Wattsie Pottsie said, "I didn't mean you. Not after what you did. Let's go, Dinah."

Dinah hesitated. "I guess I won't this time. Not if Letty can't."

Wattsie Pottsie gave a shrug, which dismissed us both and walked royally away.

"Wanna swing?" asked Dinah.

"Do you really want to swing? With me, I mean?" I asked doubtfully.

"Sure."

"Okay."

I didn't want to swing, but I was so grateful that Dinah wasn't treating me like the other kids, I would have done anything she asked.

Momma felt beholden to Dinah, too. That means she felt like we owed Dinah something. She had never been beholden to anyone before, and she didn't like it one bit. I think that's why she decided to start a 4-H club.

"How would you like it if I was your 4-H leader this year?" she asked me in the spring.

"But I thought I would be going back to Mrs. Chilton's club." I had already had one year of 4-H with Mrs. Chilton, and I knew how to bake biscuits and sew aprons.

"Under normal circumstances, you would have. But I have a reason for wanting to start a club myself." Momma paused and then made her big announcement. "I want to ask Dinah to be part of it."

"Dinah? You're going to ask Dinah to come over here?"

"I've been thinking a lot about her lately. She's been a very good and loyal friend to you, and I feel bad about how she and her brothers have been treated in our community. I can't change all of that, but I can do something for Dinah. What do you think?"

I started to whoop, then I stopped.

"What's the matter?"

"Dinah won't come," I said.

"And why not?" Momma asked.

" 'Cause she won't have any money to pay her dues with."

Momma smiled. "I've already talked to Asa and Idabelle. Dinah will have her dues money every week, and she won't have to count on her brothers bagging magpies to do it."

So Momma started the Busy Bees 4-H club, which was to include me, some other second-year girls that lived out our way, and Dinah. We were to meet once a week on Wednesday afternoons.

The next time Momma had us all sit around the table to write letters to Alma, I told him about the club—with Daddy's help, of course.

Dear Alma,

Guess what? Momma is my 4-H leader. She decided to have a club of her own. It's called Busy Bees. Dinah is in the club, too.

I guess Momma told you what happened in Mrs. Reigert's class. It was pretty awful. I hated having to tell on myself. I didn't like apologizing much better. I had to apologize to Dinah and the class. It was awful.

I'm going to try to do everything right, so I won't have to apologize ever again.

By the way, Momma still hasn't told the Knotts about the "Good News." My Sunday School teacher says that's what Gospel means.

Your sister,

Letty

A few weeks after I wrote the letter, I got one back. Alma had written a letter—just to me!

Dear Letty,

Thanks for telling me about your new 4-H club. I think you'll have fun with Momma as your teacher. She's a great lady, kiddo. Don't ever forget that.

And don't be too hard on her because she isn't going over to visit the Knotts family. A person can be a missionary in a lot of ways, and sometimes being a friend is the best way.

I'm sorry things have been tough for you. I know it doesn't seem like it, but you do have the Holy Ghost, even if you haven't felt it yet. Be patient, okay?

One more thing, kiddo. Get used to apologizing. You'll be doing a lot of it in your lifetime. Everybody does.

Thanks for writing.

Your brother,

Alma

P.S. Only seven and a half more months to go! It used to seem too long, and now it seems too short.

Alma was right. About Momma, at least. From the first day of Busy Bees, she was like a different person. It was the most amazing thing. Before, Momma had never wanted to have anything to do with Dinah or her family. Now she acted like having Dinah walk through our kitchen door was the most natural thing in the world.

She did some other amazing things, too. The first day Dinah came for Busy Bees, she said, "You know, Dinah, you have the prettiest hair. It would surely look nice tied back with a ribbon."

Dinah smiled shyly. "Think so?"

Momma pulled a ribbon from her sewing cabinet and a brush from her apron pocket. As easy as can be, she started brushing Dinah's hair back so she could tie the ribbon around it.

Brushing Dinah's hair didn't make it any less stringy, but it did look better. And somehow, without being mean about it, Momma managed to get a washcloth on Dinah's face and hands before the others came.

After that, whenever Dinah came over, Momma would brush her hair out, re-tie that ribbon, and hand her a washcloth. Before long, I noticed that Dinah had started washing her face and hands and brushing her hair before coming. She even washed her hair once. That accomplished,

Momma went to work on getting Dinah into a new, clean dress.

Before she succeeded, she told a lie: It was the first time I ever heard my Momma lie. When I asked her about it, she said, "I know I shouldn't have, but it was worth it."

What Momma had done was tell Dinah that Cheryl had made a dress for me, but it was the wrong size. That wasn't true. With my own ears, I had heard Momma ask Cheryl to make the dress *Dinah's* size.

Dinah put on the dress, and Momma combed her hair and tied it with a matching ribbon.

"How do I look?" Dinah asked.

"You look . . . you look . . . " I was so shocked, I couldn't do anything but stutter.

"What's the matter? Is something wrong?" cried Dinah.

"No, nothing's wrong," soothed Momma. "You look just fine."

"You look *beautiful*," I sputtered.

Dinah grinned. She fingered the dress lovingly all through our club meeting and wore it home when the meeting was over.

"I wonder how long it will take before Asa and Idabelle show up," Momma murmured.

"Are they coming over?" I asked, surprised.

"The minute they see that dress," Momma prophesied.

She was right. Just after supper was over, the Knotts pickup pulled into our yard and the front doorbell rang. I beat Lorenzo to answer the door, and sure enough, there were Mr. and Mrs. Knotts standing on our porch.

Mrs. Knotts looked pretty much like I remembered her, although it had been ages since I'd seen her. She was wearing a print dress, and over that, a print apron. The prints didn't match. But her smile was warm, and it made her whole face look lots prettier than it really was.

"Evening," said Mr. Knotts. "Are your ma and pa at home?"

"Momma is," I said, wondering whether or not to invite them in. Finally, I decided that since Momma was expecting them, she wouldn't mind if they sat in our living room. I let them in, then hollered, "Momma! We've got company!"

Momma walked into the living room with a smile. "Why Asa! Idabelle!" she said, holding out her hand. "How nice of you to come visit. Can I offer you some homemade root beer?"

"I'd purely enjoy some," said Idabelle.

Momma sent me off for the root beer, and after I brought in the glasses, she shooed me out.

The minute Mr. and Mrs. Knotts left, I ran back into the living room. "Momma!" I cried. "Will Dinah still be able to come to 4-H?"

"Yes."

"Can she keep the dress?"

"Yes. Not only that, Idabelle has agreed to let Dinah spend part of every day here, if she wants to. It's too lonesome for a young girl to be home alone as much as Dinah is."

"Won't you get tired of her if she's over here all the time?"

Momma looked at me with an odd expression. "What a silly thing to say, Lor-etta Miller! Of course I won't. I *like* Dinah." Then she picked up the root-beer glasses and carried them back into the kitchen, while I stared after her with an open mouth.

CHAPTER SIXTEEN

Momma was a pusher. The minute she decided what to do about the Knotts family, she went at it whole hog. She was real clever, though. So clever, that for a while even I didn't realize what she was doing.

For one thing, Momma took to letting me put off my chores until Dinah came. Then, just when I thought I had gotten away without doing them, she'd say, "Lor-etta! Don't forget that you have to clean the bathroom (or kitchen or living room) this morning." She always added, "Dinah can help you. It'll get done faster with two."

I'd been doing those chores for years, and I knew exactly how Momma wanted them done. Dinah didn't. Dinah didn't know spit about cleaning. I had to show her everything. Sometimes, Momma would appear in the doorway and watch. If we didn't do the job good enough, she made us do it over. Sometimes she even demonstrated how to do it right. When she was satisfied, she'd give us a treat and let us go outside to play for a while.

In the afternoons, Momma would set Dinah and me to work on our sewing. She was trying to get Dinah through all the first-year stuff and onto the second-year material as fast as she could. Dinah made her apron, all right, but Momma didn't stop there. To give Dinah more practice,

Momma had her sew some curtains and hem a tablecloth. Then she sent the curtains and tablecloth home with Dinah.

"You're pushing it a bit, aren't you?" Daddy asked Momma after I told him about it.

"Maybe," said Momma.

Toward the middle of summer, all the girls in Busy Bees started working on the demonstrations we were to give at the county fair. "You can give one by yourself, or you can pick a partner and give a team demonstration," Momma explained to us. I don't think she was surprised when Dinah and I decided to be a team. I think she was counting on it, because she had our demonstration already written out. She called it "Dishwashing with Dispatch."

"I don't want to give a demonstration on *dishwashing*," I grumbled. "That's boring."

"Do you have another suggestion?"

"Yeah. Why can't we show how to make a leather coin purse or comb case?"

"Hey, yeah!" agreed Dinah. "Then we could go visit Uncle Orvel!"

Momma wasn't too happy about that. She had gone to a lot of work writing "Dishwashing with Dispatch."

"Maybe next year," she said, handing us our copies. "Now we'll read this through, and you can start memorizing it."

I had my part memorized by the time we had gone through it twice. If you can't read, you learn how to memorize real fast.

For the next two weeks, we practiced our demonstration on the kitchen table for anybody who would stand still long enough to listen.

"Aw, do I have to?" was Lorenzo's response.

"Now Lorenzo, you know that we always support one another. You can take the time to listen," Momma replied.

Lorenzo listened, and so did Daddy and Cheryl.

Cheryl was willing to be our audience because we listened to her when *she* practiced. She was going to give a demonstration on making freezer jam.

But the best practice we had was after lunch one Saturday afternoon. Daddy had surprised all of us by bringing Uncle Orvel out from town that day. "It's been a long time since we've had Orvel out for a visit," he explained to Momma.

Uncle Orvel didn't deliver his usual line. He just said, "Hello, Faye."

"Hello," said Momma, stiff like. She wiped her hands on her apron and held one out like she wanted to shake hands with her own brother.

Uncle Orvel smiled the sweetest, sad smile. Then he opened his arms. Momma hesitated. *Hug him!* I silently commanded. I was just about to hug him myself when she got all teary. She bent down to put her arms around him and murmured something in his ear. "I know. It's all right," I heard him say as he patted her back.

Then Daddy, who was always warning Momma against pushing people too hard, did some pushing of his own.

"Why don't we invite Dinah and her family over and make a party of it?" he asked.

Momma stared at him for a long moment. Then she nodded. "Dinah, go tell your folks they're invited to dinner. We'll eat around six o'clock."

With all the extra leaves in the center of the table, there was room enough for everybody. All of us Millers were there (except Alma, of course), plus Alma's girlfriend, Connie and Uncle Orvel, and the whole Knotts family—even Bob.

Momma had us all mixed up. She put Mr. Knotts by Uncle Orvel, which suited Uncle Orvel just fine. Henry was by Cheryl, who looked a little uncomfortable about it. She didn't have to worry about talking to him, though.

Lorenzo was across from him, and the two of them talked all through dinner about reloading shells. Daddy tried to bring out Bob, but Bob ate more than he talked. Naturally, Dinah and I sat together. And Mrs. Knotts was seated by Momma.

That is, Momma had told her to sit there, but Mrs. Knotts wasn't much for sitting. As long as Momma was up serving, Mrs. Knotts was on her feet helping. When they finally sat down, Mrs. Knotts watched everything Momma did and tried to do the same.

It made me sort of sad to see how hard she tried, and how all the Knottses had made the effort to fix themselves up a bit. I guess Dinah's education from Momma was rubbing off on everybody.

After we were done eating, Momma said, "We have two girls here who are going to give a demonstration at the county fair. Since it's called 'Dishwashing with Dispatch,' I think now is a lovely time for them to rehearse."

"What? With all these dishes?" I cried.

"This will give you a wonderful chance to practice before a large audience. Besides, I don't think Idabelle or Asa have had a chance to see what their daughter is doing. Have you, Idabelle?"

"Dinah showed us some. Probably ain't the same without Letty."

Momma nodded in agreement. She and Mrs. Knotts helped clear the table and set it up with a wash pan, a rinse pan and a rack. The dishes we were going to use were stacked behind us on the counter. The water was heating on the stove. (According to Momma's script, we had to heat the tap water to almost boiling so it would sterilize the dishes when we washed them.) Clean, folded dishtowels were right where they were suppposed to be.

Dinah and I looked at each other. There was no way out.

We did a perfect job of it. Everybody clapped and Mrs. Knotts wiped her eyes on her apron. Uncle Orvel put his arms around me and Dinah. "You two are going to be the stars of the show," he said.

We were, but not in the way he had expected.

Dinah and I were feeling terrific about everything as we got up to give our demonstration in front of the judges and mothers and other 4-H'ers. We hadn't forgotten any of our props. We had our lines down cold. And we had done it so many times that we could have washed those dishes blind-folded.

One of my jobs was to talk about heating the water before starting to wash the dishes. I was supposed to put water in a tea kettle and heat it up before the demonstration started, so it would be ready to pour in the dishpan when the time came.

It was suppposed to be hot enough to kill the germs, but not hot enough to kill me.

I said my little speech and reached for the kettle. As I took it from the stove, I could hear the water bubbling against the metal sides. When I poured the water into the pan, great clouds of steam rose up into my face. It was obvi-ous to everybody, including me, that the water was way too hot. Nobody but a fool would think of putting their hands in that water.

Right then, I could have said, "And if the water is too hot, add the necessary amount of cool water."

I could have, if I had thought of it. Or if I had had any sense of humor—but I didn't. So I put my fingers right into that boiling water and continued on with my little speech.

Have you ever tried smiling while your fingers are being turned into Vienna sausages? It wasn't easy, but I kept right at it.

Dinah saw what was happening, of course. How could she miss? My fingers were red as fire and swelling. That's when she grabbed the wrist closest to her and held my hand up so that the audience could see the damage. "Letty forgot to mention that if your fingers are cooking, you can always add cold water. You just fill a pitcher from the tap and pour the amount you need in the dishpan. Or get some ice cubes and hold them in your fingers over the dishpan until they melt. That way, you can cool your fingers and the wash water at the same time."

Everybody laughed. I was embarrassed at first, but then I laughed, too. Dinah had always been able to make me laugh.

That got Dinah started. She cracked jokes right down to our last line: "Thank you for your attention." The audience seemed to like her jokes, even the judges. Dinah and I got a first place ribbon.

As we were about to leave, one of the judges said, "I guess every comedian needs a straight man." I had no idea what that meant at the time, but "Dishwashing with Dispatch" started something.

Dinah and I turned into hams. We drove everybody at our house nuts by putting on our version of everything from *Abbott and Costello Meet the Mummy* (Dinah and I saw it at the Rainbow Theater) to Classics Illustrated's version of *Tale of Two Cities*. I think Momma was glad when the bus pulled up in front of our farm that fall.

CHAPTER SEVENTEEN

Going to school didn't put an end to our comedy team. Far from it. As fifth graders, we were finally among the big kids in Pryor Creek Elementary School. All the younger kids looked up to us and followed us around—and fell for everything we did.

We loved it. And that's why we cooked up the business with the fire alarms. We really didn't intend to get old Wattsie Pottsie in trouble. But when the opportunity presented itself, it was just too good to pass up.

See, Wattsie Pottsie was a real pain that year, and it was all because of our new teacher, Miss Vanderheisen.

Miss Vanderheisen didn't look any older than Cheryl, although she worked at it. She pulled her wispy, blond hair into an old-lady bun, and she was always trying to look serious. She didn't have much luck at it. Her mouth didn't want to stay in a straight line any more than her hair wanted to stay put in that bun. The minute I saw her, I knew I was going to love her.

As for Miss Vanderheisen, she loved everybody. Including Dinah.

Dinah was different that year. Spending the summer at our house had changed her. She wasn't so shy, and because she had learned to speak right up, Miss Vanderheisen realized right off that she wasn't dumb. In fact, if Miss Vanderheisen had a teacher's pet at all, it was Dinah.

You can bet that was a shock to old Wattsie Pottsie. She couldn't believe it. It meant she was just another kid, no matter how many ruffles she had on her dress. Not being given any special attention was bad enough, but the worst part was that Miss Vanderheisen wasn't hoodwinked when it came to what Wattsie Pottsie could and couldn't do.

Well, Wattsie Pottsie figured that she was going to make up for not getting enough attention from the teacher by shunning me and Dinah. She tried to tell all the other kids, the girls especially, to stay away from us. The year before it would have worked, but this year was totally different. Partly because of how Miss Vanderheisen was treating everybody in class, and partly because of what Momma had done for Dinah.

And one more thing. In fifth grade, I was choosing to be with Dinah. Before then, I had hung out with her mostly because I was lonesome. That wasn't the case anymore. I liked Dinah. We had a good time together. The other kids could tell that, and they wanted to be part of our group.

Wattsie Pottsie couldn't stand it. She kept trying to butt in and take the show over. She'd walk right up and say in her old voice, "Let's jump rope." But instead of thinking of it as a command, the other girls would look to me or Dinah. If we shook our heads, it was no go. Same thing about practicing to be cheerleaders and acting out comic books.

It wasn't fair, I guess. We were doing the same thing to her that she had done to us, and we knew how it felt to be on the outside.

But it was delicious.

Anyway, three days before Christmas vacation, we pulled the fire-alarm prank. It happened one day when we were all in the hall between first and second bell. Our school building was set up with these little fire-alarm boxes that had a glass bar running from one side to the other. To set off the alarm, you were supposed to break the bar.

Well, we—that is, Dinah and I—were walking around from one fire alarm to the other, pressing on the bars. At least, it *looked* like we were pressing. We had drawn quite a following as we went up and down the stairs from one alarm to the other.

Our audience of younger kids was both appalled and amazed that we would dare to do what we were doing.

"What do you think? Should we try this one?" Dinah asked me.

"I don't think so. We might really set off an alarm."

"That's true. But it might not be a bad idea." Dinah grinned at the younger girls clustered around us. "We would have to go home."

"Let's see," I said. And I put my finger on the glass bar, and grimaced as if I was pushing very hard. "Doesn't work."

"Darn," Dinah said.

And on we went to the next one. It was ridiculous, but we were having fun.

Then Wattsie Pottsie appeared. She was furious to see that the spotlight she had once enjoyed was now focused on us, if only for a few minutes. She watched what we were doing from a distance, then she approached.

"That's stupid," she said.

"Probably," I agreed.

"You'll get into trouble if you break one of those."

"True," Dinah said, "but I don't think we can. They're too strong. I think that's because they're made for adults to break."

And Dinah made a show of applying great pressure to the fire-alarm bar.

"Let me try," said one of the fourth graders.

"Naw. I don't think it's a good idea," said Dinah.

"Why not?"

"Well, you *might* break it, and then you'd get into a lot of trouble."

"If you can't break it, she can't," said Wattsie Pottsie, tossing her red ringlets. They had looked all right when she was in second grade, but on a fifth-grader they looked ridiculous.

Dinah's eyes narrowed. "Could you?"

"Certainly. But that's not the point."

"What's the point?"

"To push it as hard as you can *without* breaking it. Right?"

I nodded to Wattsie Pottsie. "That's right. Want to try it?"

"Yeah, try it," came from several directions.

"Go ahead," encouraged Dinah.

Wattsie Pottsie hesitated. She was the one who had publicly challenged our position, but she wasn't sure she wanted to mess with the fire alarms.

"You're scared." It was the voice of a second-grade kid who rode our bus. He had lost his front teeth, so he said it, "You're thcared."

"I am not scared," declared Wattsie Pottsie.

"Anyway, this is getting boring," said Dinah beginning to walk away. Most of the kids standing around us shifted as if they were going to follow her.

"All right! All right! I'll show you how to do it," said Wattsie Pottsie, stepping regally up to the alarm. We moved back to make room for her. Her pale, freckled hand reached up to the alarm, poised for action. She laid one finger on the bar.

"Chicken," someone said. "You're not really trying."

Dinah and I just stood there, trying not to grin.

And Wattsie Pottsie pushed.

She really pushed.

And broke the glass bar.

And activated the alarm.

We were all standing right under one of the red alarm bells and the sound was ear-splitting. Everyone put their hands over their ears and scattered. Except Wattsie Pottsie, who was frozen to the spot, mouth hanging open. Her face was whiter than ever, and her freckles looked like pennies against her skin.

"What happened?" yelled Mrs. Reigert, who had dashed from her room. Spying Wattsie Pottsie standing stupidly under the alarm, she said, "Melanie Watts, did you push that?" Without waiting for an answer, Mrs. Reigert grabbed Wattsie Pottsie by the arm and dragged her off toward Miss Delmar's office.

Mrs. Reigert had, as usual, jumped to conclusions. Wattsie Pottsie *had* pushed the alarm, and she deserved everything she got, considering how she had treated us all those years. But Dinah and I were guilty, too.

We didn't stop to think much about that at the time. We were too busy enjoying the memory of Wattsie Pottsie's blank face. And the extra hour of recess we had that day, which was livened up by the arrival of two fire trucks and a police car.

CHAPTER EIGHTEEN

We didn't send much to Alma that year for Christmas, because he was almost done with his mission. And in February, Momma and Daddy packed their suitcases. They were going to Salt Lake City to pick up Alma.

"Two-and-a-half years," said Momma, shaking her head. "It went by so fast!"

I didn't think it had gone by fast at all. A lot had happened in that time.

He had left right after I started third grade. That year, while he walked door-to-door, I sat watching Dinah jump rope, wondering how to give her my shoes. Summer came, and he was still walking door-to-door, with no luck. Summer came, and I visited the Rock Pile and had the nightmare about being trapped inside Dinah's house.

Then it turned fall again, and he was excited: he had some contacts to teach. I was upset and angry: I had Mrs. Reigert for a fourth-grade teacher. One day, while he was teaching the gospel, I x-ed out the words in *Little House on the Prairie*.

Alma baptized, I apologized, and everything started looking up for both of us.

Before he came home in February, Alma was an assistant to his mission president. Before he came home in February, Miss Vanderheisen had helped me learn to spell one hundred words right. I was reading well enough to understand most of the captions under the pictures in *Look* magazine.

A lot *had* happened—and a lot had changed in two-and-a-half years. I knew it for sure the minute I laid eyes on Alma Miller, returned missionary.

"Letty!" he cried, scrambling out of the car. He said something that sounded funny. "That's French for 'Come here, sweetheart,'" he explained. Then he hoisted me up to give me a smack on the lips. He had to set me right back down. "You've gotten to be quite the young lady, kiddo! Or can I still call you that?"

I just stared at him.

"What's the matter. Don't you remember your big brother?"

"You . . . you look so different," I stammered.

"I'm just older," he said, laughing.

That wasn't it. He had been old as long as I could remember. When you're already old, two-and-a-half years don't show up so much. There was something different, though, something I couldn't put a name to. *I'm just imagining it*, I thought. If you can't name something, it's easy to decide it's not real.

It took me a few days to realize what it was. It was his face. It was *bright*, like there was a light bulb right behind it. It had a steady, warm glow that drew me near him. Like a campfire draws you near on a cold night.

I couldn't help wondering if that was how people looked on the outside when they had the Holy Ghost's cook fire on the inside.

One night a few days later, I went out to the barn while Alma was milking. He had taken his old job back to give Lorenzo a break. "Besides, I've got to see if I can still do it," he had said.

It was cold out in the barn, and steam rose from the milk bucket as it filled.

"Want a squirt?" he asked as I came in.

I squatted on my heels, and he hit my mouth with a frothy stream.

"Haven't lost my touch, have I?"

"Nope."

"Now, what do you want to talk to me about?"

"What makes you think I want to talk?"

"Why else would anybody come out here? It's freezing!"

I hesitated a minute, then I spit it out. "I don't have it."

"What?"

"The Holy Ghost."

Alma stopped milking. "Sure you have," he said. He pulled me down on his knee, just like he had the time we talked right before his mission.

"How do you know?"

"Because you got the gift of the Holy Ghost when Daddy confirmed you a member of the Church after your baptism."

"I haven't felt anything yet."

"You will," he said, giving me a squeeze. "Then again, maybe you already have, but didn't realize it."

I shook my head.

"I know you're worried about it, kiddo, but don't be. I was a lot older than you are now before I felt the Spirit."

He gave me another squeeze, then a little shove. "Got to get done here before Bossy gets her dander up." He started milking again, then looked up at me. "Do you want to know a secret?"

"Sure."

"Remember when we had that talk about the two things I could do in my new suit?"

I thought back. "Yeah. Go on a mission, or get married."

"Well, I practically wore the darn thing out on my mission. I've got the shiniest seat in five counties. So I'll have to get a new suit to get married in."

"You're getting married?"

"Yep. Connie and I have set the date. And then we're moving to Laramie. Connie's brother is going to give me a job in his store, and in the fall, I'll start at the university."

"Do Momma and Daddy know?" I cried.

"Not yet. I'm letting Connie tell her parents first."

"When?"

"In April. Right before conference."

"But that's just a month away."

"I know. But Connie's been waiting for two-and-a-half years. She doesn't want to wait any longer." He grinned and added, "Neither do I."

I guess Momma and Daddy expected Alma's news, because they didn't seem too upset. The next month, Momma and Connie's mother gave parties and packed boxes with pretty presents. They cried a little while they were doing it. "This time, Alma's going for good," Momma explained to me. "He'll have a wife and a home of his own. From now on, he'll only be coming here to visit."

With all Alma had to do, he still found time to talk to Bob Knotts a lot. Bob had been left out of most of the things we were doing with his family, because he was working such long hours at the filling station. It was like Alma felt he had to make up for that.

Whenever I could, I tried to find something to do near where they were talking.

"Stop spying on Alma and Bob," Lorenzo commanded when he caught me listening.

"I'm not spying," I protested. "I just like hearing Alma's voice."

Lorenzo looked at me suspiciously. "Oh yeah? What's so neat about Alma's voice?"

"I don't know."

I couldn't explain what I heard when Alma spoke, any more than I could describe how he looked to me. I only knew that something pulled me to him like pins to a magnet.

When Alma left for his mission, I didn't cry. When he got married and moved to Laramie, I cried every night for a week. But it was spring, and school was almost over, so it was hard to stay sad.

CHAPTER NINETEEN

The last day of school, Miss Vanderheisen said, "You've really improved your reading this year, Letty. I'm very proud of you. I just wish . . . "

"What?"

"I wish you and Dinah had made up with Melanie."

"Oh, that."

I guess it's understandable that the business with the fire alarm was the beginning of real problems between me and Dinah and Wattsie Pottsie. She had looked plenty stupid, standing there with her mouth open and the alarm shrieking above her. For weeks, everybody—even adults—called her "the girl who set off the alarm."

She was determined to get back at us no matter how long it took.

Miss Vanderheisen had tried everything she could think of to get the three of us to be friends. Like, she would assign all of us to help her put up a new bulletin board, or do some other project together. It didn't work. That really bothered her; she wanted everybody to be as sweet and loving as she was.

She didn't give up trying, not even on the last day of school.

"Letty, make an effort to get along with Melanie this summer, would you? For me?"

"I'll get along with her just fine," I said.

"Really?" Miss Vanderheisen's voice was full of hope.

"Sure. I never see her in the summer."

Boy, was I wrong about that.

That summer, I ended up nose to nose with old Wattsie Pottsie, because some dumbhead put us in the same cabin at 4-H camp.

I had expected to go with Dinah. Right up until the day I went over to her house to practice our demonstration, I thought we would be together. We were always together. We did our projects together. We swam together. We played house out on the haystack together. And we were doing our demonstration together.

Our team demonstration that year was "A Simple Supper." (You can tell Momma triumphed again.) The supper was stuffed tuna fish rolls, a green salad, and cherry tapioca using bing cherries that Momma had canned. Every time we practiced that demonstration, we ended up eating all the food. In less than two weeks, we were both sick of cherry tapioca, green salad, and stuffed tuna fish rolls.

We usually ran through the demonstration at our house, but one day, Momma surprised me by saying, "You're going to practice at Dinah's today. Everything you need is in this sack."

The last time I had gone down the Knotts lane was the day I had confessed to ruining *Little House on the Prairie*, so I was really surprised by what I saw. Something had been going on.

The old house was still the color of dirt and was still sagging, but the screen door had been fixed. It had been scrubbed down, too. And on the cement slab before it stood an old milk bucket filled with geraniums.

"Hey, Dinah!" I called.

Dinah came to the door. "Is that you, Letty?"

"Yeah. Here, take this sack. Momma sent me over to practice."

Dinah took the sack and stepped back so I could come into the house. I took a deep breath and stepped in.

It was real bright outside, so it took a minute for my eyes to adjust. And when they did, I blinked. And blinked again. I had been expecting the same mess I saw the day I fed the cake to the dog, but everything was different. The big room that served as kitchen and living room didn't look awful anymore. It didn't look great, either, but there was definitely a change for the better.

For one thing, it was clean. Instead of being piled high with dishes, the table was covered with a nice blue and white checked oilcloth. Its leg had been fixed; it didn't need magazines under it to keep it steady. The counters were clear, too, and the floor wasn't covered with stuff.

What really made the different was the addition of a couch and couple of covered chairs at one end. And curtains at the windows. The curtains that Momma had Dinah hem the year before.

"My gosh! What have you been doing?" I asked.

"Nothing much. Just stuff your ma has taught me."

"Momma taught you how to clean a kitchen? When?"

Dinah grinned. "When she made me help you. I've learned a lot by doing your work."

"What does your momma think about this?"

"She likes it. She gets mad at the boys if they come in with dirty boots, and she makes them help wash the dishes. Even Pa."

"Your daddy washes the dishes?"

"Yeah. We do it just like I learned from our demonstration. Except we don't boil the meat off our fingers."

"That reminds me, we'd better get to practicing," I said.

When we were through with our demonstration, we had a good green salad, a plate full of tuna rolls, and a bowl of cherry tapioca on the table before us.

"I'm glad eating this stuff isn't part of the demonstration. Yuck. Makes me want to throw up just looking at it," I said. "And I sure don't want to lug it back home. Hey, if you feed it to your family, you won't have to fix supper tonight!"

"Won't your ma mind?"

"No. Are you going shopping for camp stuff with Momma and me?"

Dinah was suddenly very still. "I'm not going to camp," she said softly.

"What? But I thought you were! We made all those plans—"

"I can't. I've got to be cook and housekeeper around here."

"Can't you be gone for just one week?"

"No."

"If it's money—"

"I can't go, Letty." Dinah's voice was muffled, and I could tell she was crying.

"I don't want to go without you."

We put our arms around each other. "You go," said Dinah. "You'll have fun. And you can tell me all about it when you come back."

I agreed, but inside, I didn't accept it. And when I got home, I cornered Momma.

"Why didn't you tell me Dinah couldn't go to camp!"

"I just found out about it myself," said Momma.

"Well, make her folks let her go!"

"I can't do that, Letty. It's a matter of pride for Asa and Idabelle. You know, they've never missed giving Dinah her 4-H dues—not once. And they've paid for all the material and supplies she's needed. It hasn't been easy, but they've done it. But a whole week of camping is too expensive."

"Why can't you trick them into letting her go? You tricked them into letting her keep the dress last year. You tricked Dinah into making curtains for their kitchen. You even tricked her into learning how to clean house."

Momma nodded soberly. "I know. And that wasn't right, Letty."

"Why not," I wailed.

"Letty, listen. When I did those things, I thought I was doing right. But I wasn't showing any respect for them or their feelings."

"Who cares? It worked!"

"I know it did, and I'm thankful for that. But Letty, I'm not going to manipulate either Asa or Idabelle into doing something they don't feel right about doing. And they don't feel right about letting someone else pay for Dinah's camp."

"Then I don't want to go, either."

"We've already sent in the form and money, Letty. Besides, you need the experience. A few days apart from Dinah won't be the end of the world."

I sure felt like it was the end of the world as I trudged up the trail to the tent cabin I had been assigned. No one else from the Busy Bees was going to camp, so I had to bunk with a bunch of total strangers. Or so I thought until the moment I walked through the tent flap and found myself staring at Wattsie Pottsie. Someone had assigned me to the tent cabin occupied by her 4-H club. And in her club, Wattsie Pottsie was queen.

There was no doubt I was in enemy territory. I didn't get any hangers or a shelf to put my stuff on, and I was stuck on a bottom bunk. I sat on it and watched Wattsie Pottsie preen for Gloria Nesbitt and Janet Banks and other girls from my class at school.

There wasn't one of them that I liked, and the feeling was mutual. No matter where we went or what we were supposed to do, I was shoved aside. I tried not to let it matter, but it did. Dinah wasn't around to make me feel better, and being an outsider wasn't any fun.

They ignored me until it was time to get ready for bed. I was right in the middle of taking off my shirt, when one of the girls yelled, "Look! Letty's got a bra!"

I did indeed have a bra.

A few days before camp, Momma had taken me into town to get the things I needed. We picked up a little tube of toothpaste, a plastic soap case, a flashlight and batteries, and other stuff like that. But when I thought we were finished, Momma had a surprise for me.

"Let's go see about getting you a bra."

Startled, I looked first at Momma, then down at my flat chest. "A bra?" I asked.

"It's time," she pronounced.

Momma had me try on bra after bra, but they were all too big. "Well, we'll just have to make a little alteration," she said.

That very evening, she sat down at her sewing machine and sewed my bra flat along the seam line. And I mean flat.

"There. Try that on," she said, handing me the ridiculous harness.

It didn't do much for my ego that the cup now fit just right.

"Now you wear that bra every day at camp," Momma commanded.

"But why? I don't really need it."

"Yes, you do. Just do as you're told," she finished.

And I did.

Now, I was surrounded by girls, and they were all pulling at the bra. Suddenly, I felt the hook in the back give, and someone pulled the bra right off me. I clutched my shirt to me as Wattsie Pottsie held my bra up triumphantly.

"Give that back!" I yelled.

"I don't know," smirked Wattsie Pottsie. "I think maybe I'll wear it tomorrow."

"And me the day after that," someone cried.

"Then me!" insisted Gloria Nesbitt.

That was enough. I lunged for my bra, and managed to catch onto one end of it. Wattsie Pottsie pulled on the other and the tug-of-war began. We would have torn that bra apart if the leader hadn't walked in. "What is going on in here?" she demanded.

Wattsie Pottsie let go of her end of the bra. Not a person moved. No one spoke.

"Whose bra is that?" asked the leader.

"It's mine," I said.

"What exactly was going on?"

I opened my mouth, fully expecting to tell on Wattsie Pottsie. I was as surprised as anyone when I said, "Nothing. I told Wa . . . Melanie she could wear it tomorrow."

"What?"

"You know, she wants to try wearing one. Besides," I added with a little grin, "she needs it more than I do." And I handed the bra to Wattsie Pottsie.

At first she looked at it like it was a snake, then she took it.

"Okay, now into your bunks," ordered the leader.

The next day, Wattsie Pottsie wore the bra. The day after, it was passed on to Janet and then to Gloria. By the time the week was over, everyone had had a turn wearing my bra. It was considered a prize by everyone in the cabin. Why, without me and my bra, camp wouldn't have been any fun.

For the first time in years. I felt the warmth of Melanie's approval and the safety of being part of a group. It was wonderful. So wonderful, that when school started in the fall, I didn't want to give it up.

But Melanie didn't want anything to do with Dinah. I had to make a choice—and I chose Melanie.

Melanie smiled.

CHAPTER TWENTY

Dinah was miserable, I could tell. Lots of times, it looked like she was about to cry. She stopped participating in class. She sat by herself in the cafeteria and squatted in a corner of the building during recess. Whenever she managed to get close enough to me to ask me what the matter was, I always said, "Nothing."

When Joe asked me why I didn't sit by her on the bus anymore, I said, " 'Cause I don't feel like it."

When Momma said, "I haven't seen Dinah lately. Is she sick?" I mumbled something about her being busy.

That answer didn't hold Momma for long. A few days after school started, Momma steered me into Daddy's office. "All right. I've talked to Idabelle, and I want to know what's going on here, Lor-etta Miller!"

"What?" I asked innocently.

"You know exactly what I'm talking about."

I tried to play dumb, but I couldn't meet Momma's eyes.

"What's happened between you and Dinah?"

"Nothing."

"Don't play games with me, young lady."

"I'm not. Nothing's happened. I just want to do things with some of the other girls for a while. That's what you always wanted, isn't it?"

"What do you mean?"

"I can remember a time when you didn't want me to have anything to do with Dinah."

Momma looked at me sharply. "That was a long time ago, Lor-etta. A lot of things have changed since then, and you know it."

I shrugged. Momma's eyes got wide, and I could tell she was real mad.

"What is it with you?" she demanded.

"I want to be like everybody else, for once!" I blurted out. "I want to be part of the group! I've never been part of it, not once in my whole life. When Dinah and I got to be friends, it was just two outcasts getting together. Nobody wanted either one of us around. Momma, I want to be just a plain, okay person for once in my life."

Momma sighed. "I understand. But that doesn't mean you have to ignore Dinah, certainly."

"Yes, it does! If I'm with Dinah, I'm out."

"Letty, do you know what this is doing to her?"

I ducked my head. "I don't care."

That wasn't exactly the truth. I cared enough that I never looked at her straight on. The hurt in her eyes made me feel too guilty. At the same time, I was furious at her for not standing up for herself. I wanted her to spit in Melanie's eye the way she always had. And mine too, for that matter. I wanted her to be tough and strong. I wanted her not to need me that much.

Sometimes I found myself wondering how it was going to end. The way things were going, I was afraid something terrible might happen. I thought about apologizing, but it wasn't like the business with the book in fourth grade. I hadn't really done anything wrong.

Had I?

It all came to a head one day during recess. As usual, Dinah was huddled in the "inny" corner. As usual, Melanie and her crowd—including me—were stuck together in a clump. We were talking about bras. I was still wearing mine, despite the fact that I really didn't need it. Several others had begun wearing them too, although they didn't need one, either.

"The only person in our class who really needs to be wearing a bra is Dinah," said Melanie. Her lips curled nastily when she said Dinah's name.

Everybody turned to look at Dinah.

"She sure does," Gloria commented.

"I wish I looked like that," said Janet.

Dinah had been looking at her shoes. Now she raised her eyes and saw us all staring at her. She looked so sad that I felt like shaking her. *Get up!* I cried silently. *Fight!*

But Dinah just crouched in the corner.

I'll make you fight! I thought grimly. *I'll give you something to fight about.*

And I blurted out, "Dinah wears falsies."

"What?" gasped the group in unison.

"Are you sure?" asked Melanie.

"Of course, I'm sure."

"Falsies," snickered Janet. "Bet she wears them just so she can get the boys interested."

"I think we ought to make her tell," decided Melanie.

"Let's!" agreed everyone but me. I didn't say anything at all.

The group moved toward Dinah, who seemed to know something awful was going to happen. But she was already in the corner, so there was no place for her to run.

"What do you want?" she whispered.

"We want you to show us your falsies!" said Melanie.

Dinah's jaw dropped. Nothing came out of her open mouth.

Stand up! I urged her in my mind. *Hit Melanie. Hit me!*

But Dinah didn't move. Except for her eyes. They turned to me and for a long moment, we looked at one another. Then she started to cry.

And I turned and ran.

When the bell sounded the end of recess, I entered the building reluctantly. Slowly, I walked to the sixth-grade classroom. I was trying to figure out how I was going to get to my seat without having to look at Dinah.

I didn't have to worry. Dinah wasn't there.

She wasn't on the bus, either.

"Where's Dinah?" I asked Henry when he got on.

"Why do you want to know? Haven't you made her feel bad enough?"

"I *have* to know. She wasn't in school all afternoon."

Now Henry looked worried. He stood up and headed for the door.

"Where are you going?" I cried.

"To the laundry."

Of course. That had to be where Dinah had gone: to the laundry, to her momma.

Somehow, I kept from crying all the way home, but I let go the minute I got off the bus. Tears were blinding my eyes as I ran out to the barn where I knew I would be alone, except for old Bossy. In the protection of the musty darkness, I sobbed for a long time. I never knew a person's heart could hurt so bad.

I had done something terrible, that was the truth of it. And there was nobody I could blame for it but myself—not even Melanie Watts.

Melanie!

No, not Melanie. *Wattsie Pottsie.*

"You dumbbell!" I cried as the realization hit me. I kicked the side of the manger so hard that I had to hop on one

141

foot for a while. Old Bossy's brown eyes watched me as she chewed her cud.

"I've been taken for a ride!" I yelled at Bossy. "Wattsie Pottsie's made a fool of me. She's been looking for a way to get back at me and Dinah ever since the fire alarm. She knew there was no way to hurt either one of us as long as we were together. She *knew* that! That's why she was so nice to me. That's why she let me into her group."

Old Bossy's silence encouraged me to talk on. As I talked, things got clearer and clearer.

"She's a smart one, Bossy. She had it all figured out. It was perfect. She got *me* to do her dirty work. She knew I would, because I wanted to be a regular person. I wanted to be safe. And I thought being part of her group would do that.

"What a joke," I continued bitterly. "Dinah's worth the whole bunch of them. *And I have to tell her!*"

I scrambled out of the barn and ran as fast as I could along the ditch at the top of the alfalfa field. But when I got almost to her house, I slowed down. I had no idea what I was going to say, and I was afraid that Dinah would hate me no matter what I said.

For the first time in years, I whispered a prayer.

A while ago, back when I gave up on the Holy Ghost, I'd stopped saying prayers except when it was my turn to bless the food or say family prayer. I didn't think there was any reason to. Now, I prayed as hard as I could. Then I walked the rest of the way to Dinah's.

Nobody was home. I sat down on the cement slab to wait. I wasn't going to leave until I had begged Dinah to forgive me. I waited a long time. The sun was low in the sky, turning the clouds pink and purple, before the Knotts family's pickup turned onto the lane. I stood up as the pickup came to a stop.

Silently, they climbed out. Mr. Knotts emerged first, followed by Mrs. Knotts, Henry, and finally Dinah. Dinah's eyes were red and puffy, and there was so much hurt in them I started to cry myself. Mrs. Knotts put her arm around Dinah like she thought I was going to do something awful.

Finally Mr. Knotts spoke. "Didn't think you would ever hurt my little gal. Not you."

"I didn't mean to," I cried. The words sounded limp and useless.

"Maybe you better go," he said.

"Please! I made a mistake. The worst mistake of my whole life. I'm sorry! If it would make you believe me, I'd cut off my hand!"

I waved my right hand dramatically, but it made no impression. Dinah buried her face into her momma's side. The others stared at me with cold eyes.

"Oh, please!" I cried again. Then I crumbled. I bawled so hard and so long that Mr. and Mrs. Knotts got scared that I might make myself sick.

"You get ahold of yourself, girlie," Mr. Knotts said. His voice wasn't so hard anymore. "Pick yourself up, and I'll drive you home."

"I don't want . . . to go home. Not until Dinah forgives me."

"Well, Dinah, it's up to you. Guess you'll have to forgive her, or I'll have to pitch a tent over her head."

I dared to raise my eyes then. Dinah was looking at me from the protection of her momma's arm. I met her eyes, and I felt her look go right through my eyes into the very middle of me.

Make her see I'm sorry, I begged the Lord. I'll never do anything bad again.

I guess Dinah knew what I was thinking. She took a little step forward and I ran into her arms.

CHAPTER TWENTY-ONE

Dinah forgave me right then, but it didn't mean she trusted me. None of the Knotts family did; I could tell by the expression in their eyes. It was the old coyote look: wary and hurt. And when Mr. Knotts drove me home, he didn't say a word until he pulled up to a stop by our sidewalk. Then he said shortly, "I'm comin' in with you."

Momma met us at the door. "Asa! Is everything all right? I was worried when Idabelle phoned and asked me to send you into town."

For an answer, Mr. Knotts pulled me out where Momma could see me. "Letty! I wondered where you were, young lady. Did you and Dinah make up?"

I looked down at my saddle shoes as Mr. Knotts said, "This gal's done a right mean thing to my Dinah. You ask her about it." He was about to leave when he added, "I think maybe ya'll ought to keep to yourselves for a spell."

"What? Asa!" cried Momma, but he didn't respond. Momma stared at him as he got in his pickup and drove out the gate. Then she turned to me and demanded, "Loretta Miller! What have you done!"

This time, I couldn't get away with acting like I didn't know what she was talking about. I had to come right out and tell her. It wasn't easy; I was afraid she would get mad.

But she didn't. She just got sadder and sadder the more I tried to explain.

Finally, I ran out of things to say. "I only wanted her to fight back," I whispered. "I couldn't stand seeing her act like a wimp."

"What you mean is, you couldn't stand seeing how much your behavior was hurting her."

I wiped my tears away with the back of my hand. "Momma, I don't want Dinah to feel bad. She's the best friend I ever had. I went over to apologize, but I don't think it did any good."

"Doesn't seem that way. You've got a tough row to hoe in front of you, Letty. We all do."

I don't think any of us realized how much we would miss having Dinah and her family around. More than once Momma started a sentence with "Dinah . . . " and then stopped. More than once I saw Daddy leaning against the top rail on the corral, staring off toward the mountains. More than once Lorenzo went out to the garage to load shells, only to wander back a few minutes later.

"Aren't you going to reload?" Momma would ask.

"Naw. It's no fun alone," he'd say.

And more than once I cried myself to sleep at night.

"This is ridiculous," said Daddy one day. "I'm going over there."

"Are you sure that's what you want to do?" asked Momma. "Asa and Idabelle might not welcome you. They've been hurt, Orrin, and they won't want to show it. They're proud people."

"All right, I won't go. But it seems like that's been the problem all the way around, hasn't it? Pride."

Momma sighed.

So we missed them when they weren't around, and we were miserable when they were.

Like when we rode the bus to school. I refused to go with Joe over the bump anymore, and Momma didn't make me. When I stopped catching the bus on the way out, Joe stopped too.

"What's going on?" asked the bus driver the first day that happened. Nobody said anything. He looked from the Knotts kids to us Millers and back again. "Oh. Having troubles, are you?"

Dinah and Henry were sitting together in the middle of the bus. Joe and I sat down in the front—quickly, so we wouldn't have to meet their eyes.

As bad as riding the bus with Dinah was, being in the same class with her was torture. She was pleasant enough, but she never talked to me unless I asked her something. She didn't come to where I was during recess—I had to go to her. Sometimes, she didn't play with me at all. She found other kids to play with, and I don't mean Wattsie Pottsie and Company.

After I told Wattsie Pottsie to take a flying leap, she tried to recruit Dinah. Dinah wasn't taken in by her flattery, though. She understood Wattsie Pottsie all too well. Besides, she didn't need Wattsie Pottsie. There were other kids in our class who were glad to play with her, and there was a whole passel of younger kids who still thought she was wonderful.

That left me pretty much on my own. I cried a lot at first, then I started to do just what Dinah was doing. I looked for other kids to play with, and to my surprise I discovered they were easy to find. There were almost thirty kids in our class, and Wattsie Pottsie only claimed eight or so. That left a lot of kids who were also looking for friends.

It was strange. It was like Dinah and I had been Siamese twins, and somebody had separated us. We were finding out that we both had what it took to stand on our own two feet.

Still, I missed her. Our whole family missed their whole family. Cheryl had gotten so used to Dinah that she thought of her as a little sister.

"Why don't you just invite them over?" Cheryl asked Momma one night.

"I'm afraid they might not come."

"But they *might*."

Momma considered. I could tell what was going on in her head by the way her face changed expressions. At first, she was feeling sad. Then she was thinking: Maybe it would work. Maybe they would come. After that, she had scared thoughts: Maybe they *won't* come. And then she got tough. I could see it in the way she set her jaw.

"I'm going to ask them," she said to Cheryl. "The worst they can do is say no."

They said no.

"Give them more time," said Daddy.

"Pray about it," wrote Alma, who had started college at Laramie that fall.

"Why did you tell him?" I asked Momma. "I didn't want him to know!"

"I didn't. Connie's mother did."

"Great. The whole town knows."

To me, Alma wrote: "Remember way back when I told you that people end up apologizing all the time? It's nothing to be ashamed about. In fact, it takes courage to apologize, and I'm proud of you. I just hope you can figure out a way to be friends with Dinah again. You two are quite a pair."

Alma's letter made me feel better, but I wasn't sure what good apologizing had done. It hadn't fixed things, like it did the first time. Two whole families were miserable, all because of me. It was a pretty big burden for a twelve-year-old. But Alma had said we should pray, so every night I prayed, "Father in Heaven, help our families to be friends again."

It didn't seem to do much good. Every time we bumped into any member of the Knotts family, it was awful. Like the time Daddy and I walked into the Shoe and Saddle Shop and found Dinah and Mr. Knotts there.

"Well, if it isn't my favorite bunch of people in the same place at the same time," said Uncle Orvel after greeting us.

There was a dead silence. Dinah looked at her shoes and Mr. Knotts said, "Are you about done with that boot, Orvel?"

Uncle Orvel eyed us all with those steady brown eyes of his. Then he said, "Sure. Here it is. Just had to sew up the seam, so it's only twenty-five cents."

Mr. Knotts paid Uncle Orvel.

"Say, if you've got other business, I've got some time. Letty and Dinah can work on a project if they want to."

More silence.

Daddy cleared his throat and said, "Asa, this isn't any good—"

"Thanks, Orvel," Mr. Knotts interrupted. Then taking Dinah's hand, he walked out of the door.

"Whew! Are you two feuding?" asked Uncle Orvel.

"I never thought of it that way, but I believe you're right," said Daddy.

"That doesn't sound too good. Where Asa comes from, feuds are serious."

"I know. What I don't know is how to stop it."

"Let me think on it a bit," Uncle Orvel suggested.

"Be my guest," said Daddy.

Uncle Orvel was already thinking when we walked out the door. I could tell because his eyebrows were drawn together, and he was resting his chin on the back of his hand. It looked like he was propping up his nose with it.

"What do you suppose he'll do?" I asked Daddy.

"I don't have the faintest idea, kiddo," Daddy said.

A few days later, the phone rang at our house. Momma answered it.

"Why, hello Orvel . . . You what? . . . Since when do you invite people to dinner? . . . Of course, if you really want to, we'll be there."

Momma hung up the phone. "Orvel's invited us all to dinner Saturday night. Can you imagine that?"

I looked at Daddy, and he grinned. It was a little grin, and Momma missed it.

Well, Saturday night, we all trooped into the Shoe and Saddle Shop just before closing. Uncle Orvel got down from his stool.

"Here's my company," he said to Buck. "You'll close up?"

"Yep, if you're sure you don't need me around to help put out the fire when you start cooking."

"I'm sure."

When Momma has company for dinner, she starts cooking hours ahead of time, and the whole house smells good by the time the company gets there. Uncle Orvel hadn't done a thing. I know, 'cause I sniffed and sniffed, but there was no smell of food in the air. The table wasn't set. It didn't look like he was expecting company at all.

"Orvel, can I do anything to help?" asked Momma. She was trying to be subtle .

"Nope. Why don't you all take a seat."

We did. The conversations ran in fits and starts, just like our John Deere had been running since Mr. Knotts stopped working on it. Uncle Orvel had a funny, listening look on his face.

"Are you expecting someone?" Momma asked.

He just shrugged. But a moment later there was a knock on his back door. He opened it and in walked the Knotts family. They stopped dead still when they saw us. We looked at them, they looked at us, and for a moment nobody said a word.

"Orvel Pryor!" said Momma finally. "I should have guessed you were up to something." But she wasn't mad. Her voice was soft and she was smiling.

Mr. Knotts was standing at the head of his family. He wasn't smiling. By his right shoulder stood Mrs. Knotts and Dinah. They weren't smiling either, but they weren't mad. The boys were back by the door staring at their feet.

"Did you know about this, Idabelle?" Mr. Knotts asked his wife.

"No," she said in her soft drawl. "But Asa, even if I'd-a known about it, I wouldn't-a stopped it. We cain't go on like this. This ain't the Smoky Mountains. We ain't feuding—"

"Ain't we? Our gal here has been insulted. That means we've all been insulted."

"But I apologized!" I cried. "Isn't that enough?"

"I know about your apologizing, Loretta."

My heart sank when I heard my name so stiff and formal. Uncle Orvel's idea wasn't going to work. We would be enemies forever. I felt Momma put her arm around me, and I turned my face into her shoulder so nobody could see my tears.

"Come on, Asa," pleaded Daddy. "We've been friends for a good many years—"

"We've been neighbors," corrected Mr. Knotts.

"For most of those years, that's true. But things have been different these past months. We're not just neighbors anymore. We care for each other more than that."

Mr. Knotts started to leave.

"Hear me out, Asa," asked Daddy. "It's one thing for two grown men to decide they are going to hold a grudge, but it's not fair to pass that on to both families. It's for sure not fair to the girls. Letty did a mean thing and that's a fact. She's ashamed of it, and she's apologized for it. But there's not much more she can do if you won't give her the chance. She needs time to show she's sincere."

Dinah tugged on her daddy's hand. "Please, Pa," she asked softly. "Can't we be friends again?"

"Let them, Asa," said Uncle Orvel. "And let us be your friends. We want to."

Mr. Knotts looked around at his family. They didn't say anything but I could tell by the expression on their faces that they wanted him to make peace.

"There's no code of honor here that says you have to fight," Uncle Orvel added. "None of us wants to, least of all me—unless you give me an advantage."

He looked up at Mr. Knotts, who towered over him. Then he grabbed a chair and put it in front of Mr. Knotts. Before anybody could guess what Uncle Orvel was going to do, he climbed up on it.

"That's better," he chortled. "At least now we're eye-to-eye, wouldn't you say, Asa?"

Mr. Knotts got red in the face. At first, I thought he was mad, but then I realized he was trying not to laugh. "You took a mighty big risk asking us to come, Orvel," he said in a funny voice.

"That's true," Uncle Orvel said, climbing down from the chair and putting his hands on his hips. I could tell by his grin that he thought the feud was over. "But I'm short, you see. I figured if the bunch of you started fighting each other, I would just get down on my hands and knees, crawl between your legs, and get out quick!"

Then Mr. Knotts did laugh, a great bellowing laugh that burst right out. Before you knew it, everybody was laughing. Momma and Mrs. Knotts were hugging each other. Daddy and Mr. Knotts shook hands and slapped each other on the back. Cheryl and Dinah and I put our arms around each other and danced in a circle. The boys just grinned and shuffled from one foot to another.

When the ruckus calmed down a bit, Daddy asked Mr. Knotts, "Did Orvel invite you to dinner, by any chance?"

"That was the idea, but I don't see no victuals. Don't smell none, neither."

"Orvel," said Daddy, "You may have invited us here for some reason of your own, but we're all hungry. Aren't you going to feed us?"

"Sure, but I had to plan for two different outcomes of this little venture," explained Uncle Orvel. "I didn't know if I could get you people to stop ignoring each other, so it hardly made sense to fix a big meal if there was a chance I'd end up eating it all myself. On the other hand, if my plan did succeed, I knew you'd hold me to my invitation. So there was only one solution."

"Which was?" asked Daddy.

"Pancakes!"

Uncle Orvel headed for the cupboard. "Well, come on, Faye," he said over his shoulder. "You did offer to help."

Momma and Mrs. Knotts fell in behind him, arm-in-arm. Spirits were high as Uncle Orvel put sausage on to cook and Momma and Mrs. Knotts started making the pancake batter. Before long the whole apartment was full of good, warm smells.

They were the best pancakes I ever ate.

CHAPTER TWENTY-TWO

Dad was right about it taking time for things to get back to normal. Except for Momma and Mrs. Knotts, we all needed time to figure out how to act around each other again.

A couple of weeks passed before Mr. Knotts came over with his toolbox to help Daddy fix the old John Deere. A few more passed before he and Daddy leaned up against the corral, looked out over the field, and chewed their toothpicks like they used to.

Same with Henry and Bob. It was one thing for them to come over with cartridges to reload. It was another to shoulder their guns and go pheasant hunting with Lorenzo. He was surely glad when they finally did.

Dinah and I, we started off pretending that nothing had ever happened. We sat together on the bus and played together at recess. She helped me out with my reading when I needed it. And I helped her with her math—even when she didn't need it. I guess I was showing off a little because I could figure out the problems quicker.

But something had happened, and one day when I was bossing her around, Dinah exploded.

"What makes you think you can always say what we're going to do?"

"I—"

"Maybe I don't want to swing, did you ever think of that? Of course not! You never think about anybody's feelings but your own. Well, I have feelings, too! And you hurt them, a lot!"

"What are you talking about?"

"You know."

"I thought that was all over and done with—"

"Well, you're wrong. When it happened, I just crawled in a corner and sucked my thumb. I was sad then and for a long time after. But now, I'm mad! I'm going to tell you something and you better listen."

"I'm lis—"

"If you ever do something like that to me again, I'll . . . I'll push your nose in the dirt! Got it?"

I nodded, speechless.

Dinah stomped away, then turned and stomped back. "Now shall we swing?"

I followed her over to the swings, amazed at how tall and strong she looked as she strode out ahead of me. For a long time, I had secretly felt that Dinah was lucky to have me for a friend. Right then, I felt lucky to have her for a friend.

The rest of my sixth-grade year was pretty dull. When Stevie McClenahan and Billy Bucher started teasing me and Dinah, things livened up a bit, but there really isn't anything else to tell. Except maybe about the last day of school and the cake Dinah brought.

Our teacher, Mr. Thomas, decided that we should have a party the last day of school. He assigned everybody to bring something. I was supposed to bring a salad, and Dinah was suppposed to bring a cake.

By then, Dinah was real good at making cakes. They were always tall and moist, just like the 4-H cookbook said they were suppposed to be. She was good at making fancy frosting, too. When Momma invited Uncle Orvel and

Dinah's family to Easter dinner that year, she asked Dinah to make one of her cakes. That shows you how good she was.

Dinah went all out for our party. She made a three-layer devil's food cake and frosted it with tons of swirly sour cream and chocolate frosting. When she took the wax paper off that cake, the whole class groaned in anticipation.

Melanie Watts had made a cake, too, but Dinah's cake was the one everybody wanted. Dinah sliced it in thin pieces, but it still didn't go far enough. The kids who didn't get a piece begged a taste from the ones who did.

They made such a big fuss over it that I began to feel a little sorry for Melanie. Her cake wasn't all that bad, it just wasn't spectacular. The more I thought about it, the stronger I got the feeling that I should ask Melanie for a piece of her cake.

Finally, I couldn't sit still any longer. "Hey, Melanie," I called. "Cut me a piece of your cake, will you?"

"Sure! How big a piece do you want?"

Melanie's bright smile and too-loud voice got to me. "That cake looks real good," I said, loud enough for everybody to hear. "I bet I could eat a big one."

Melanie cut a piece for me and one for herself. We sat down together at the back of the room, eating the cake and watching Dinah. She was still surrounded by kids, even though her cake was gone right down to the last crumb.

"This is great cake," I said.

"Thanks!" Melanie said, smiling at me.

I smiled back at her. Then I looked up. Dinah was watching us, and she had a smile on her face, too.

The party marked the end of our years in Pryor Creek Elementary School. The next fall, we would be going into junior high school. We would practically be grown up.

Dinah and I talked a lot about it during the summer. We made plans about all the things we would do together. It never occurred to either of us that Dinah and her family might not be living on the Rock Pile when the first day of school came in the fall.

The move came as a total surprise. I didn't have any idea what was going on until the day Daddy said, "Guess Asa and the family will be moving into town now that he's got a job at the John Deere dealership."

"Orrin, did he really get it?" asked Momma, wiping her hands on her apron.

"Yep."

"Wonderful!" Momma said.

"What do you mean move to town?" I asked. "And what's this about Mr. Knotts having a job?"

"Well, you know how I always brag to the dealer about how Asa keeps my old John Deere running. Seems Gregory got tired of hearing it. He finally decided that if Asa was as good as all that, he'd offer him a job. But first, he wanted to see what Asa could do."

"And Asa impressed him?" asked Momma.

"Knocked him off his feet. I've always said the man was a genius with machines. And listen to this. Gregory not only gave Asa a job, he offered to rent him that nice little place over on Third Street. Asa's talking it over with his family right now!"

"I'm so glad, Orrin. That means Idabelle won't have to work at the laundry anymore."

"Means Bob won't have to drive so far—"

"What it means," I interrupted, "is that Dinah won't be living right next door!" And then I started to cry.

"You'll see Dinah every day at school, just like always," Momma assured me.

"It won't be the same! What about summer?"

156

"You can invite her to sleep over. And sometimes you can stay with her overnight in town."

"It won't be the *same!*"

"Sometimes it's best that things don't stay the same," said Momma. "You don't really want Dinah to stay on the Rock Pile. Do you?"

For a long time, I couldn't say anything. I was thinking about the nightmare of so many years ago. I had an idea how Dinah might have felt living in that house—and I could imagine how she would feel about leaving it. *If* I didn't ruin it for her by being selfish.

I shook my head. "No. I don't want her to stay."

"Then be happy for her, sweetie."

"I am."

Dinah's family moved a few days before school was sup-popsed to start in the fall of 1957. Their new house was ready for them, and every Knotts and Miller had the blisters to prove it. We got some of the blisters while waxing and polishing the hardwood floors in the living room and dining room. The others we got scrubbing cabinets and washing windows.

You know how Momma likes things just right? Well, she decided that we had to make curtains and tie matching quilts for all three bedrooms. At the same time, she wanted to help Mrs. Knotts get acquainted with her new neighbors. So after we had run up the curtains, Momma invited those ladies to come out for lunch and an afternoon of tying quilts.

All the time we were doing those things, I knew that Dinah was going to move. But knowing didn't prepare me for how I felt the day I walked the familiar route along the top of the alfalfa field to say good-bye. Dinah was only going into town, but it felt like she was going to Utah or

Colorado or some other place that was at the end of the world.

Too soon, we loaded the last things in the pickup. Mr. Knotts locked the front door of the dirt-colored house, and it was time for Dinah to say good-bye.

"Good luck," I said, hoping nobody would notice that my chin was bouncing. I shook hands with Mr. Knotts and then with Mrs. Knotts. When I came to Henry, I sort of socked him on the arm. "Guess you'll have to give up shooting magpies, huh?"

"Maybe. But I'm planning on going bow hunting with Lorenzo in the fall."

Then only Dinah was left. We looked at each other, then we both burst into tears.

"Land sakes," said Mrs. Knotts. "Y'all don't need to carry on. School starts soon, and you'll be seeing each other every day!"

Dinah and I laughed a little sheepishly through our tears.

"That's it," said Mrs. Knotts, putting an arm around each of us. "I want to thank you, Letty, for being such a good friend to my girl here."

I ducked my head. "I wasn't always."

"Maybe not," said Dinah, "but I always knew you loved me."

I stared at her in a moment of shocked recognition. Dinah was right. I did love her. As I hugged her, my tears were replaced by a smile.

I was still smiling as I started home. I felt so good, I couldn't help skipping and singing. Then I stopped dead still as a sweet warmth flooded over me. It settled nice and steady in my heart, and I knew right off it was like the kind of fire that doesn't burn fried potatoes. It made me stretch out with love for the whole world. I would have hugged the world if I could have, but since I couldn't, I hugged me instead.

That's when it came to me, so clear and right that I knew it was true: In learning to love Dinah, I had learned to love myself.

CHAPTER TWENTY-THREE

The last Saturday before school started I asked Momma, "Can I get penny loafers this year instead of saddle shoes?"

I asked the question without much hope, but to my surprise, she said, "I don't see why not."

"When can we get them?"

Momma reached into her purse and pulled out a ten-dollar bill. "Here. You can ride into town with Lorenzo whenever you want to."

"You mean you're not coming shopping with me? How come?"

"Letty, I've been going school shopping for eighteen years. I'm tired of it. Besides," she added, "I think you can do all right on your own."

I was overcome by sudden doubts. "Are you sure about this?"

"Sure I'm sure." Momma smiled and smoothed my hair, which was kinked-up, as usual.

The next morning, I put on my least grubby pair of socks and rode into town with Lorenzo, who was driving in to get a part for the John Deere. He dropped me off in front of J.C. Penney. After I finished buying my shoes, I was supposed to meet him at Dinah's house.

Never since Momma bought me my first new pair of shoes had I been so excited about shopping. I couldn't help grinning to myself as I walked back to the J.C. Penney shoe department.

"Can I help you, young lady?" asked the man.

"I want some penny loafers," I said proudly.

"What size?"

"I don't know. I grew a lot in sixth grade."

"Take off your shoe and we'll check."

I unlaced the saddle shoe on my right foot and took it off. I was ever so glad that the sock, while not as wonderfully white as the promises in the Tide advertisement, didn't have holes in the heel.

The man put my right foot on the metal sizer and announced "A size seven should fit you just right."

Then he got a box from the back room and took out a penny loafer. Holding a shoehorn behind my heel, he slipped my foot right in it. I stood up and wiggled my toes. There was plenty of room. I walked around to make sure my heel wouldn't slip out, and finally stood in front of the short mirror to see how it looked.

The reflection in the mirror showed two feet, one in a beautiful, rich brown penny loafer (which was still minus the penny) and the other in an old, scuffy saddle shoe. Right then, I knew I'd never wear saddle shoes again.

"I'll take them," I said.

"Do you want to try on both of them?"

"No."

"Do you want some anklets?"

I hesitated. "How much do the shoes cost?"

"Seven ninety-five."

"Then put in two pair of anklets."

The man had taken the penny loafer off my right foot. He put it back in the box and rang up the sale while I put my saddle shoe back on.

I was triumphant as I left the store. When I went to junior high in the fall, I would be wearing penny loafers!

And maybe a touch of Tangee lipstick, if I could get away with it.

For some reason, I didn't try on the other shoe until later on that evening, after I had shown them to everyone and had retreated to the upstairs bedroom. Cheryl had already left for college, so the attic room was now mine. In the delicious quiet and privacy, I opened the box. Instantly, the smell of new leather filled the air. I put on a pair of the impossibly white anklets and then, with the help of the shoehorn, put on the shoe I had tried on earlier in the day.

Without the slightest hesitation, I slid my toes into the left shoe, then put the shoehorn behind my heel and pushed. My toe bumped into the end of the shoe, stopping the forward motion before my heel had a chance to slide down into place. I pulled my eyebrows together and pushed again. And again. Then I got panicky. Throwing the shoehorn aside, I pulled and tugged.

It didn't do any good. The left shoe didn't fit.

It never occurred to me that the fault might lie with the man in the J.C. Penney shoe department, that he might have put the wrong size shoe in my box when cleaning up at the end of a day. I didn't even think to check the sizes.

I was devastated. I had gone to town that morning full of excitement, and I had purchased my shoes with joy, but I had done it wrong. I had thought I was getting over that. I was better at reading, and I was real good at cooking and sewing. I was always a whiz at math. But it seemed that there was another mystery nobody had let me in on: how to buy shoes.

That made me mad. I pushed my foot into the shoe again and yanked—hard. The little leather edging in the back of the shoe ripped away, but my foot slid in.

"That'll show you!" I muttered. Never mind that threads were hanging from the torn edging and that my toes were crunched together. I had both shoes on.

"Letty, what are you doing?" called Momma from the kitchen.

"Trying on my new shoes."

"Come show them to us."

Now I was going to get it. I sighed. *I might as well get it now as later,* I thought as I walked down to the kitchen. Momma was still at the sink and Daddy was sitting at the table reading the paper. Lorenzo was gluing feathers onto the arrows he was making for bow hunting in the fall.

"Well?" I asked, standing self-consciously in the doorway.

"They look nice, dear." That was Momma.

"Umhumm," Daddy agreed.

Lorenzo said, "When are you going to put the pennies in?"

"As soon as I clean some with Momma's copper cleaner."

And that was all. Nobody even noticed that I was standing a little funny, or the ruination of my left shoe. I was a little disappointed, to tell the truth. I didn't want to get yelled at, but it would have been nice if somebody had paid enough attention to notice.

They never did find out. The next time we went to town, I sneaked my shoes in to Uncle Orvel.

"How would you like to be laughed at?" he asked me.

"I will be laughed at if you can't fix my shoe." I held out the mutilated penny loafer.

"This shoe looks new. What happened to it?"

I told him.

"Let's see what I can do," he said.

He moved the light right over the big sewing machine and bent to his task. In a few minutes, he had sewn the edging back on the left shoe. He was about to put a wooden form into the shoe to stretch it, when he asked, "What size do you wear, Letty?"

"Seven."

"Let me see that other shoe."

I handed it to him, and he looked inside it. Then he looked inside the left shoe.

"You tried on the right shoe, didn't you?"

"Yes."

"And not the left?"

"Not in the store."

"Well, your problem is simple, sweetie. This shoe (he held up the right one) is size seven. *This* shoe is size six-and-a-half."

"What?"

"It's the wrong size shoe. You really ought to take it back."

My mouth dropped. The thought of facing the man in the shoe department was mortifying.

"You wouldn't get into any trouble," Uncle Orvel assured me. "After all, they have another box of shoes with mixed sizes. They'll probably be mighty grateful to you for straightening the situation out. Besides, now that I've sewn this one up, it looks good as new."

"I don't know . . . "

He slid down from his stool. I was lots taller than he was, now, but when he took me by the hand, I felt little again. "Come on. I'll go with you. Buck, if anyone comes in, tell them I'll be back in a minute. Got some business to do."

"Sure enough," said Buck.

"Let's get at it," said Uncle Orvel, motioning me out the door. "Don't want you going to school limping like me."

I could have hugged him right then, and I wish I had, but we were already out on the street, and I was afraid that someone would see us.

Uncle Orvel got things straightened out easy as pie. He knew the man in the shoe department. He called him Duane.

Duane just laughed and went behind the curtain into the back where all the shoes were stored. In a few minutes he came out holding another box in his hand. "Think we've got it," he said. "You sit right down here, young lady. We're going to try on both shoes this time."

He took the right shoe from the box we had brought in and slipped it on. The left shoe he took from the box he had fetched from the back room. He put the shoehorn behind my heel, and I gave my foot the slightest shove. It went right in.

"Now walk around a little. How do they feel?"

"Just right!"

"I sure thank you all for coming in and taking care of that little problem. We want our customers to be satisfied."

"Just one more thing," said Uncle Orvel. "You're a mighty good storyteller, Duane. But don't go making a story out of this."

Duane looked at me, and I blushed. "Don't worry, little lady. I won't."

"Thanks," I said.

"Do you still have some time?" asked Uncle Orvel when we were back on the sidewalk.

I nodded. "Dinah's not expecting me for fifteen minutes yet. Why?"

"Come on back to the shop and you'll see."

When we got back, he got out some cream he had and polished up two pennies. "Give me your shoes." I did, and he put the pennies in the little slots. Then he handed me a can of brown Kiwi shoe polish. "On the house," he said.

That's when I did hug him. There were some people in the shop looking at saddles and stuff, but I didn't care.

I was wearing those shoes proudly when Momma took our picture the day I was to go into seventh grade.

As we were lining up, I told Momma, "I'm too old to ride over the bump anymore."

Momma smiled. "You don't have to. Joe can catch the bus on the way out himself if he still wants to."

Joe's face fell. I wondered if that was the way I looked the day Lorenzo told me he wasn't going to ride over the bump anymore. I reached out and tweaked his ear. "Doesn't mean I won't play Scrabble or Chinese Checkers with you. I'll still be your pal."

The reason I didn't want to catch the bus on the way out was that I didn't want to see the Knotts place looking empty and abandoned. It never occurred to me that the people who were renting the Rock Pile might have already moved in.

That's why I was so surprised when I got on the bus. Besides Joe, there were three little kids sitting on the green seats. I knew right off they had to be the kids of the people who were renting the Knotts place. First, because there wasn't another stop beyond our place except Dinah's old house. Second, because there was a look about them . . .

There were three of them, all grade-school age. The boys were sitting together. Someone had tried to cut their blond hair but hadn't done a very good job of it. Both of them had been skinned above the ears and the hair left on top stood out like a thatch. Neither had taken time to wash their hands or face before getting on the bus. One had some duck mud in his eyes and the other needed to wipe his nose.

The little girl was sitting alone in the seat behind them. She looked like she was about seven or eight years old. She had long, brown hair that was matted from not being combed. Her bangs hung down into eyes that looked too dark in her colorless face. She was wearing a blue dress that was too big. On her feet were dingy anklets that were sagging at the heels, and saddle shoes that looked just like the shoes Dinah had been wearing that day in second grade when I wanted to trade with her.

I stared at her for what was only a second but seemed an eternity. Tears gathered in my eyes and my nose began to sting. It wasn't just the saddle shoes that got to me. It was the look in her eyes. I saw in them the same hungry, scared, sad look that I had seen in the faces of Dinah and her brothers when I got on the bus for the first time six years before.

"Sit down, Letty," Lorenzo said, still giving me orders.

I looked down the aisle to where Joe was sitting on the back seat. He motioned to me, but instead of going to sit by him, I slipped in beside the little girl. Without thinking much about it, I crossed my ankles and tucked my feet under the seat where my new loafers with the brightly winking pennies would be out of sight.

"Hi," I said. "My name's Letty. What's yours?"